ASTERIUS

A TIMELESSNESS NOVELLA

Susana Imaginário

ISBN: 978-1-7398202-8-2 (paperback)

Also by Susana Imaginário

The Timelessness Series

Wyrd Gods
The Dharkan
Nephilim's Hex
Anachrony
Anamnesis

Related to Timelessness

Oublié
To Trick a Trickster
Daemons

I

My name is Asterius, yet I have never seen the stars.

I was born in darkness, deep in the dungeons below the grand palace of Knossos in Krete, and put in a cage before I even drew breath. I am the product of lust, deception and spiteful vengeance – the favourite weapons with which the gods like to fight amongst themselves. My mother was queen Pasiphaë, a daughter of Helios, the Titan of the sun, and wife of King Minos.

My father was a bull.

Many believed this unthinkable indiscretion had not been her fault. That Eros, the cruel god of love, provoked her lust for the animal with his arrow. But it is also known that gods and their scions have unusual proclivities. Her sister, Circe, for example, enjoyed turning men into pigs. Maybe the kink ran in the family. Who can tell? Lesser deities, desperate for attention, are prone to such things.

People called me a monster because I'm half man and half bull. Although I've often wondered which part is the most monstrous… And since I'm no ordinary beast, no ordinary cage would do to hold me either, so King Minos had Daedalus, the best architect, designer and inventor the world had ever seen – and the closest thing I came to have as a father – build the greatest maze ever created, a prison to rival Tartarus in the Underworld.

They called it The Labyrinth.

There I lived my entire life. However long that was exactly, I cannot tell you. Time has no meaning or purpose in the dark. For darkness existed long before the advent of time and will continue after its end. My purpose was simple, though. It's the purpose common to all monsters: to be hated, feared, bound and then slaughtered so weak men can appear brave, strong and righteous. They'd come to Krete from all over the Aegean and beyond, intent on killing me – a feat that would turn them into heroes.

I refused to oblige them.

Krete was renowned as the birthplace of Zeus, king of the Olympian gods and the cause of most of their problems – yes, of course, you of all gods know that. As I said before, his lust was not responsible for my birth. But that doesn't mean he was not instrumental in my fate. Many would say, in fact, that it all started when my cousin Medea enchanted Talos – the giant automaton Zeus commissioned of Hephaestus to protect the island – allowing Jason and his argonauts to destroy it.

Deprived of his island's main defence, King Minos prayed to Poseidon for assistance. In answer, Poseidon sent the most magnificent white bull anyone had ever seen under strict instructions for it to be sacrificed in his name. Maybe you can explain why the god of the sea would send a bull, of all creatures. I cannot. And I cannot fathom what went through the king's mind when he decided to keep the bull for himself either. Did he actually think he could cheat Poseidon with the sacrifice of a lesser specimen? Perhaps he did. Kings, much like gods, tend to think themselves above all others. I suppose they are in a way. And, as Daedalus liked to say, the taller you stand, the less you see.

Such a wise man, Daedalus. Too wise for a mortal, the gods would say. I asked him about the bull once, when I was still a boy, struggling to understand how or why I came to be. He told me that Poseidon was a better judge of humanity than all his siblings combined, and he relished punishing their hubris.

I see that you agree... He's your brother too, isn't he? Well, back then I was too young to grasp the full meaning of Daedalus' reply and I thought little of the gods, who'd made me this way. I thought even less of humanity for treating me so unfairly. For why was *I* being punished? I never asked to be born, to be immortal or immortalised. I never wanted to kill. Never wanted to hate or be hated. I only yearned to live and be free. To see the sky. The sun! Failing that... I wanted to be left alone. Which I supposed I was – most of the time.

You say you can relate. Perhaps you can. Yet you don't really care, do you? You only care about my death, not my life. But I cannot tell you one without telling the other, so you'll just have to bear with me.

That day I felt, rather than heard, the arrival of the fresh batch of Tributes sent to die by my hand. Most were already searching for me. For if they killed me, they would not only gain their freedom but fame as well, their names and deeds remembered for eternity. And mortals will do anything to become immortal, even if only in name.

Their quest was doomed, of course. Even armed – each tribute was allowed to carry one item, and most chose a weapon – they were no match for my size, strength, experience and knowledge of the maze. Yet they still tried, for what had they to lose? Their lives had been forfeited the moment they entered the Labyrinth. Just like mine had been at birth, I suppose. They were all destined to die without ever seeing the sun again. With me. Like me…

I should have gone to them immediately. Spared their misery. Such was my duty, after all. My function. My curse… I should have embraced it, been the villain I was meant to be. For no matter how many of them I killed or how many times they failed to kill me, I'd never be the hero. I'd always be the monster and they, my victims. And yet I was never able to commit to the role, to fulfil it wholeheartedly.

On that particular day, I remember being filled with apathy, on the verge of melancholia. Killing, always unpleasant, had become trite. I was weary of it, bored with it. More than anything, I was sick of their hatred, their fear, their prejudice. Tired of cleaning up their blood and their waste. Of dragging their corpses into the pit that ran to the sewer, of watching them wash away. But above all, I was tired of their noise.

Humans make so much noise – all the time. I could hear them up in the palace and all the way down to the river through the ventilation shafts and drains. Always shouting at each other. Stomping about. One would think they were the ones with hooves for feet!

Me? I'm quiet as a snake, as you can attest. And just as despised, I suppose…

My room – or den, if you prefer – was a large dome at the centre of the Labyrinth with a blazing hearth, and there I stood, listening to the noise of the seven men and six women trapped in the maze with me. I remember thinking that was strange, an odd count. Tributes always came in batches of seven males and seven females. No, not all those sent below were aspiring heroes. Many were just unfortunate, petty criminals caught in the wrong place, at the wrong time, by the wrong people. And the vast majority of Tributes were slaves, sent to the Labyrinth as both offerings to gods and levies to the king. For in the Aegean, life was cheaper than gold.

But they were always given a choice: either drown in the ocean or enter the Labyrinth. Funny how many chose the Labyrinth. They feared Poseidon more than me.

I can tell by your expression that you understand why… Yes, tell me later.

Anyway, I figured the odd count meant that after two decades of monthly Tributes, Krete had to be running low on thieves and prostitutes, murderers, outlandish priests and general undesirables such as, you know, anyone who dared call their king a crook or a cuckold, for example.

On that particular day, I had no motivation or inclination to fight. Still, a fight broke out in the darkness, nonetheless. By the sound of it, some of the men were trying to rape the women. This happened a lot. Away from judging eyes, the condemned often sought one last pleasure, heightened by cruelty, before the end. Sometimes they even began killing each other, saving me the trouble.

Humans do the stupidest things when they think

they can get away with it, or that they have nothing to lose if they get caught. Once, a bunch of sailors tried to force themselves on a group of Amazons. By the time I got to them, they begged me for death. Amazons don't fuck around in a fight, you see. I still bear a scar from a spear one plunged into my thigh. A good thing her aim was off in the dark. Another time, a priestess of Artemis, and as crazy as they come, hunted and skinned each man one by one – alive. She almost succeeded in hunting me down as well! Imagine that. Such a vicious creature… Otherwise, I might have spared her. Let her do all the killing. Yet another woman, this time a priestess of Aphrodite and the most beautiful female I'd ever seen, tried to seduce me. She claimed to worship me, to desire me the way my mother desired my sire. Fool that I was back then, I let her get close, and she nearly gouged my eye out with a chisel.

I was young. Vulnerable to both lust and praise. No, it wasn't that unusual for women to try to seduce me, hoping to be spared long enough for an opportunity to slay me, but wanton flesh never really interested me, especially not after that one.

Of course, I could have taken any woman by force if I wanted to. And I cannot say I haven't been tempted on occasion. But I have my pride. I might be a monster, but I'm not monstrous. And let's not forget, I myself am the product of rape – even if Mother did most of the raping.

Gods play under different rules, and when it comes to their lust, not even animals are safe. Am I wrong? Didn't think so.

As I was saying, by the sound of things, those women were no fighters, hunters or seductresses, and the men were likely to take what they wanted from them. I decided to put an end to it. For even if they were whores, they deserved a say in the matter, did they not?

I moved silently through the long corridors and winding angular intersections I knew so well until I was just a few steps away from the group, and once there, I roared like the beast they expected to find. I had often tried a more sensible, less degrading approach, but it always resulted in confusion, bordering on dismay. These humans expected a monster: a bovine, brainless creature making guttural sounds. So that's what I gave them. I did whatever it took to get the task over with as quickly as possible.

I huffed and puffed as I stomped in their direction, roaring like a bull in chains. As intended, the men paused in their attack on the women and turned to face me. They couldn't actually see me in the dark, so they just stood there, eyes wide and blind, waving their pitiful weapons in the air.

It never ceased to amaze me how few actually had the sense to bring a light source. Unlike them, and after a lifetime in gloom, I could see well enough in the dark, but I'm no cheat. Nor am I a fool, mind. They deserved to see me before I killed them, but to bring a flame would have given away my approach. Always the wisest, Daedalus had provided me with an alternative. One of his greatest inventions: the dynamo torch.

You're not familiar with it? Er, I'm not sure I can explain how it worked, exactly. Let's see… In a nutshell, the device generated light from motion and friction. I know, truly ingenious.

I squeezed the handle and began to spin the flywheel

attached to its generator. The grinding sound of the mechanism seemed to scare the humans more than any roar I could produce, which I suppose was why the torch itself never became popular. Like so many of Daedalus' marvellous inventions, it was too weird, too complex, and its function too 'sorcerous' for the average human mind to grasp.

White light began to flicker within the glass tube. The humans gasped. First at it, then at me. Their faces wore identical expressions, no matter how dissimilar the features: shifting from awe to terror until they settled on rage. I put the torch down slowly and gave out my best snort. They reeked of filth and fear and a dozen other foulnesses. But above all, malice. For they were allowed to hurt me, you see. They saw it not only as a means to survive but as their moral right to kill the beast. And the only way I could defend myself was by becoming one, thus proving them right.

Monsters can't afford to be heroes.

The first man – a pockmarked specimen with a self-righteous attitude – came at me with a club. I took it from his hand and punched him square in the face. I felt his nose fracture against my fist. The next one faltered, cringing at the wet snapping sound – the last thing he heard before I smashed in his skull with the club. The third one kept his wits about him and dodged my blow, vaulting past me in the narrow corridor. Stars, he was fast. So quick, spry and nimble, I reckoned he must have been a thief or an acrobat. He feigned an attack, then slipped past me again, practically running along the wall as he plunged a dagger between my ribs. The pain seared through my flesh into my core.

He lunged again. This time I sidestepped, sending him flying chin first into the wall with a backhanded blow. He fell to the ground, spitting broken teeth, and I crushed his head with my hoof, bellowing in rage as well as agony.

The fourth one witnessed all this frozen in place, shaking. He'd pissed himself. Disgusted, I kicked him in the chest, piercing his heart with a broken sternum.

The fifth turned to run and stumbled into the sixth. Both fell in a tangle of limbs, kicking, punching and cutting each other with near identical shivs. They looked alike, too. I reckon they must have been brothers to behave like that. I shook my head and picked up the club again. Usually I prefer an axe, but the blunt, bludgeoning weapon was growing on me, I have to admit. Sadly, it shattered against the back of one of the men. The impact sent another stab of pain through my side. I groaned.

The men stopped fighting to shout curses at me. Fools. As if I'd not been cursed enough already. I kicked and stomped on them both until they fell silent and still. The last man had not waited around to watch all this. He'd gone to hide with the women. They screamed at him to go away, revealing their location. I picked up the now fading torch and spun it back to life while I ran to them. Normally I wouldn't – run, I mean. Slow and steady steps add so much more depth and gravitas to their dread. But I was in no mood for chasing Tributes. I was wounded and angry and I wanted to end this quickly.

The women had backed themselves into one of the many dead-end corners of the Labyrinth. The man stood in front of them, holding a hatchet. He threw it at me – a pitiful throw if ever there was one. I caught it by the handle in midair and, without breaking stride, buried it in his skull. He fell to his knees, cross-eyed, an expression of utter bewilderment on his moronic face. Then he emptied his bowels and tumbled to the side.

The women screamed in earnest now. Stars, such loud creatures they were. Did I say men make noise? Women are worse. They'd mastered the arts of pleading, weeping and shrieking. I suppose that due to the limitations of their physical strength and social status, noise was all they could do. Still, my side hurt. My head ached. I had no patience for that shit.

"Please!" one said with tears in her eyes.

"Spare me, I beg of you," said another.

"I have children!" the first one claimed as if it mattered.

"I'll be your slave," said a half-starved one who clearly had never been anything else in her life.

"I have money!" the fattest one wailed. Likely that had been the answer to all her problems in life until now.

I'd heard it all before, countless times from countless mouths. Sometimes they even sounded convincing. I knew better, though.

The two less vocal women held each other against the wall, praying to any god who might listen. I pitied them the most.

The eyes of the one who'd claimed to be a mother turned to the hatchet, still protruding from the man's skull and within her reach. I took a step back and extended a hand, inviting her to take it. She did not hesitate. Her hands were on the handle even before I lowered mine, and she pulled at it with all her strength, grunting with the effort for all the good it did her. She was too weak, the blade buried too deep in the bone. Finally, she relented and sobbed, "Mercy…"

I gave her the only mercy I knew, the only mercy available for me to give. I grabbed her scrawny neck and broke it cleanly under the horrified gazes of the others. Her death was fast and painless. The same for the rest of them.

It is done, I thought and drew a deep breath in preparation for the next task: cleaning up the mess.

I checked my wound. As I feared, it bled profusely. The bastard had twisted the blade. I had to tend to it first, and fast. The corpses weren't going anywhere.

I was about to return to my den when I heard a rustle and a moan. One of the men, the first one I'd hit, still breathed. I groaned in vexation and trudged back to where the fight had begun. Sure enough, there he was, clutching his ruined nose. His eyes bulged, and he gurgled something when he saw me, then he screamed – or the closest thing to a scream uttered through a mouth filled with blood. Another heavy punch to the face finished the job.

"*Now*, it is done," I said, resigned rather than relieved.

I headed back to the dome, but just as I sat down to tend to my wound, I caught a fresh scent in the air: tangy and briny like the sea. We were close to the ocean, so I smelled it often through the ventilation shafts, but that had not been the direction the wind blew that day. Besides, there were hints of herbs and wood smoke to this scent. I cursed, realising someone – likely a seventh woman – was still out there, lost in the maze. I cursed again and stomped my hoof, frustrated with my careless optimism and lack of zeal. Minos always sent seven males and seven females to the Labyrinth. Why would it have been different this time? Daedalus always said a rushed task doubles the work. He was never wrong. I had to find her and kill her. Couldn't just let a human roam free in the Labyrinth alone for days, without food or water, destined to die slowly and miserably. I'm not that kind of monster. Well… not unless they really piss me off, that is.

Er… I'd rather not talk about it. It's not relevant to this story.

…

You really want to know? All right.

Once, a man covered himself in shit, thinking it would make him less appetising, and when I got close, he threw faeces at me. I felt such disgust, both at his actions and at the idea he actually believed I ate human flesh, that I just left him there, alone. It took him nearly six days to die of thirst, this after he'd drunk his own piss and even licked condensation from the stone walls until his tongue bled. Then he sucked on that, too. Oh, don't look so appalled. I bet you've seen and done much worse. Besides, you asked me to tell.

I had no intention of letting it go that far this time. It's just that right then I really couldn't be bothered to go chasing after the woman. I figured the next day would be soon enough. Much like the corpses, she wasn't going anywhere.

Once settled, I lit up the main lantern, not caring if the light drew the stray Tribute there – that would actually make things easier for me – and inspected the cut. It was bad, the bleeding even worse than I'd initially thought. I remember thinking, *Forget about the light. She'll be able to track me here just by following the blood trail.*

Never before had I been dealt such a wound, and let me tell you, I did not care for the experience.

My grandsire was a Titan, as I already stated at the beginning of this tale, and you well know it to be true, which meant I had enough ichor in my veins to make me immortal – so long as it stayed in my veins, that is. Otherwise, much like Talos, who was not even alive to begin with, I would die.

Wretched as my life was, I still had no wish to experience the Underworld – no offence – so I pressed a cloth against the wound and bound it as best I could while I waited for Daedalus to come. He always checked on me after a Tribute, to make sure situations like this hadn't happened. He would be so disappointed in me… Between the injury and the escapee, this had been by far my sloppiest work. On top of everything, that realisation drained the rest of my mood. I lowered my horns in shame, staring at the polished stone floor, immobile. And I waited.

II

I was almost asleep when I heard the hushed call.

"Asterius?"

"Icarus?" I had not expected him and he was not who I needed to see. I shuffled closer to my only means of communication with the outside world – a small opening in the wall that connected the Labyrinth to the dungeons – and drew back the curtain. "Where is your father?" I sounded disappointed, almost reproachful. It's not that I was not glad to see Icarus, it's just that the boy, as talented and well intended as he was, had no skill at healing.

The strain in my voice must have given away my pain, for the boy seemed to understand this. "He couldn't come," he said apologetically. "A lot's happening up there." His eyes glanced at the ceiling, then back to me. "What… er, what happened down here? Are you hurt?"

"Yes. I need stitching." Might as well have said I needed sunlight. The boy's arms were long enough to reach through the aperture and his hands dexterous enough to work a needle – unlike mine – but he fainted at the mere sight of blood. A curse from the gods, or the weakness of a sheltered mortal. I cannot tell.

"Oh… I'm sorry. I – Er… I can try," he suggested, already growing pale.

I forced a chuckle: half laugh, half groan. "It's all right," I lied. Then sighed. "Did you bring food?"

He perked up. "Yes! Plenty. Wine too! I figured you'd be hungry, after, well…" He left the sentence unfinished and passed me a bundle of fresh fruit, nuts, bread, cheese and boiled eggs.

That's right: no meat. Have you ever met a carnivorous bull? The idea that I feasted on human flesh was nonsense, for I'd sooner eat beef than long pig. And I preferred cheese and fruit to pretty much anything else. So there!

Why did I eat at all? I don't know. I just did. Don't you? There you go, then. May I continue?

My mouth watered at the sight of fresh figs, and despite the pain, I let out an appraising sound at the unexpected treat so early in the summer.

"Figured you'd be happy to see those," Icarus said. "Father's experiments with sand and limestone are working. He says one day every town will have a glass house and we'll be able to eat any fruit we want, any time of the year."

I grunted in appreciation as I chewed the sweet fruit. It was said Krete had been blessed by the gods. That it had better crops, wine and weather than any other island in the Aegean due to the sacrificed Tributes. It might have been true. The gods do like to reward cruelty. But I knew Daedalus and his inventions had as much, if not more, to do with the island's bountifulness.

"So, what *is* happening up there?" I asked between bites.

The boy deflated again, eyes darting from me to the apple he held in his hand without much enthusiasm. He was fourteen. Not quite a child, not yet a man, and thin to the point of gauntness. Like his father, Icarus spent a lot of time with his head in the clouds and treated the needs of his living body as a hindrance. He often forgot to eat and when he did, it was out of necessity, not pleasure or appetite. To aggravate things, he'd become extremely aware of his weight since he'd got it in his head that humans should be able to fly like birds. He'd been working on a set of wings for that very purpose. The way I saw it, if he got any lighter, he would not need wings at all, only the wind.

"Oh, where to begin…" He nibbled the fruit and sighed as a man resigned to an unpleasant task.

"The beginning," I grumbled through a mouthful, sounding very much like a ruminating beast.

"Androgeus is dead," he said matter-of-factly.

I shrugged, indifferent to the news. The prince – my half-brother – was a few years older than me, but a life of pampering and self-indulgence had left him immature and soft. In order to prove himself worthy of his father's throne he'd set out across the sea to Athens, determined to kill my sire – the white bull – who now, after having been tamed and ridden across the Aegean to the mainland by the hero Heracles, spent his days terrorising the plains of Marathon. Or more likely just grazing, but people scare easily and are prone to exaggeration. In any case, Androgeus claimed he wanted to avenge the queen's honour. But like many young men before him and many still to come, what he'd truly wanted was to achieve fame and immortality. Well, seemed like he achieved neither.

"I guess he did not kill my sire, then," I said, not entirely displeased.

"No. Quite the opposite," Icarus replied cautiously.

I ate another fig and said, "You can't blame a beast for self-defence." *And yet they blame me*, I thought. Of course they did. I'm not a mindless beast. I just happened to look like one. And Minos knew it.

Icarus nibbled on the apple for a bit before he spoke again, more to the fruit than to me. "Another has killed the bull. I'm sorry, Asterius…"

I waved away his condolences. I had no tender feelings for the creature who sired me. I'd never even seen him. I doubt it would make any difference if I had. A bull is a bull is a bull. Sent from the sea by a god or born in a field, it made no difference.

Many believed Heracles should have killed the poor animal when he had the chance, instead of taking him away to new pastures. It had been what Minos had hired him to do, after all. But Heracles was a true hero, a demigod, son of Zeus. Killing came easily for him, and so it had become a chore. He chose to spare the animal and had a bit of fun instead. I could relate. Though I secretly hoped the bull had put up a fight against the one who took his life.

I waited for Icarus to swallow another morsel of apple.

"His name is Theseus. The hero who killed the white bull," the boy elaborated unnecessarily.

"Never heard of him." Not that I heard much of

anything down there. But I knew my history. Daedalus took a personal interest in my education. He used to tell me stories about the gods when I was little. Later, he taught me to read and count. He taught me about the stars, the different worlds, and those who ruled them. I knew more than I cared to about gods and kings, their kingdoms and heroes, so I was surprised by my ignorance.

"No one has heard of him until now. He claims to be the illegitimate son of King Aegeus of Athens, Minos' greatest rival." Icarus paused his explanation to spit out a seed. "Or Poseidon. His mother isn't sure."

"How can she not be sure?" I asked.

"She claimed both the king and the god, er... took her on the same night."

I snorted in derision. "Sure. When in doubt, why not pick both god *and* king? I bet she's a princess."

Icarus nodded. "Aethra, the only daughter of King Pittheus of Troezen, a kingdom so small and remote Minos himself didn't know it existed until now."

I shook my head. It made sense. Women like her were common both in the stories and in real life. They wanted fame and power as desperately as men, but their options were much more limited. They could either marry a king or give birth to one.

The boy leaned in closer to the wall and whispered. "Apparently King Aegeus – before he was king, that is – stopped on their shore during the return voyage from..." He looked at the apple as if to find the answer written there. "Bah, I forget. It's not important. What matters is that he's admitted to the deed, and he's boasting to anyone who cares to listen that Poseidon was so jealous of his conquest, he took his sloppy seconds."

"Clever," I said sarcastically. If there's one thing the gods won't tolerate, it's hubris. Then again, what did I care about the fate of a king across the sea? It only amazed me how vain and stupid men like him could be. Likely this little princess couldn't get a husband – not one to suit her ambition, that is – and upon learning a 'real' prince had landed on her shore, she did what little princesses do best and offered herself to him as a great gift. Then Aegeus did what vainglorious princes do: He opened the gift and left, leaving her with a gift of his own, a child. Under such circumstances, the default solution is always to blame a god.

The stars know gods like to plant their seed far and wide, but I doubt even Zeus is responsible for half the offspring royal women have claimed to be his. I said as much out loud to Icarus.

He laughed. "Father said the exact same thing. The fact remains that the boy grew up believing he is both the rightful king of Athens, Troezen, *and* a son of Poseidon."

"Modest," I said, genuinely astounded by the exorbitance of such claims. To be fair, raised by a woman like Aethra, anyone would grow up thinking himself special. To even entertain otherwise would crumple their egos.

"Not at all," said the boy, for whom sarcasm often went unnoticed. "He's arrogant and vain. An insolent creature of violent passions. But he has reason to be. He's killed a beast, and that makes him a hero."

"Humph. Doesn't take much to become a hero these days," I said.

Icarus swallowed the last morsel of an apple. "Takes the same as it always has: the people's desire to make one."

"Ain't that the truth," I grumbled, too low for him to hear.

"After Androgeus failed, Aegeus, who has no legitimate sons as you know, promised Athens to any man who killed the bull," the boy continued. "Not only would it solve him the problem of succession, it would provoke and humiliate Minos, something the Athenian king never ceases to do. As you can imagine, Theseus could not be more perfect for the role. And whatever else Theseus is, he's not stupid. He's quick of both body and mind and he knows things. He showed bravery and initiative by killing the bull. And he has a way of captivating people of all walks of life with his handsome looks and quick smile. After he'd completed the deed, Aegeus was more than happy to acknowledge the bastard."

"Good for them," I said sardonically, growing bored. Tales of heroes are all the same, especially after being passed on and exaggerated by dozens of mouths eager to share them, each adding a little bit of their own fancy to the story. I sat back against the wall, leaving the rest of the meal untouched as pain and annoyance overcame appetite. I'd have to cauterise the wound, something I'd really rather not do but should have done already. I groaned, letting the idea settle in before I spoke again.

"Well, no wonder there's such a commotion up there. The prince is dead and Aegeus has not only gained a son but a hero to boot. Minos must be furious. Someone's going to have to pay for it." Fury is often a king's manifestation of heartbreak. And their grief is seldom placated without some kind of bloodshed. War was inevitable.

It's not my problem, I decided.

I was about to thank Icarus for the food and bid him farewell so I could get on with my dreadful task when I noticed his silence. Something prickled my mind then. My eyes narrowed in suspicion. Had I not been distracted with pain and slow-witted from blood loss, I might have picked it up sooner. "Why are you telling me about Theseus? How do you even know about all this?"

Icarus looked more pained than I felt. He bit his lip, and it was as if I heard his words before he spoke them. "He's here, Asterius. In the palace. Theseus, he… he's come to kill you."

My ears twitched despite myself.

"Not right now!" Icarus assured me, seeing my distress. "But he's determined to do it. He claims that it's his fate to end yours."

I must have looked pretty stunned by this, not to mention alarmed at the prospect, for I was in no condition to fight anyone right then, especially heroes. "Surely Minos is not taking him seriously," I said rather apoplectically.

"Oh, he is. Very much so. He's encouraging it, in fact."

"But I am his pet, his prize – his *Taurus*," I said, unexpectedly outraged by the idea the king would want to dispose of me. "I am the symbol of his power. The beast he uses to intimidate his enemies and punish his subjects!"

"And he has very few of those these days. People are starting to resent the demand for Tributes. To fear even coming to Krete in case they get arrested. You are too good at your job," Icarus pointed out with the innocent wisdom of the young, then frowned. "What happened, by the way? How did you get stabbed?"

I forced out a breath. "A thief caught me off guard. My fault. I underestimated him."

"Bad time to be injured…" said the youth.

"You think?!"

"Yes. They'll likely send more soon: soldiers – not thieves – along with Theseus."

Of course they will, I thought ruefully. "Is the hero not hero enough to kill me on his own?"

Icarus smiled in sympathy. "He's not like Heracles. He doesn't fight fair. Theseus tricked the bull in order to kill it. Taunted him to exhaustion. He's…" The boy twisted his mouth in distaste.

"What?" I asked, getting frustrated with his hesitations.

"Father says he's soulless."

"There's no such thing."

"I'm not so sure. I looked into his eyes, Asterius, and… there's nothing there but greed."

"Greed is something."

"I suppose…" He trailed off. Then suddenly cheered up. "Don't worry! You still have a few days to recover and prepare, with the wedding and all."

My ears perked up. "Whose wedding?"

"Minos is giving away Ariadne's hand in marriage to Theseus – before the fight. That way, if Theseus loses – which Minos still believes he will – the princess will have a claim to the throne of Athens. And if he wins, Minos gets to replace his dead son with a living hero as a son-in-law."

"Ah…" Things started to make sense now. "And Theseus agreed to that?"

"Sure. Theseus believes he's going to win. And he's the sort of man for whom one kingdom is not enough. He wants to rule the entire Aegean, even if he has to kill every monster and marry every princess on every island to achieve it."

I tsked. "Poor Ariadne."

Icarus laughed. "Not at all! She's over the moon. Completely besotted with Theseus and the idea of becoming the most prestigious queen in the world."

Poor Ariadne, I said again to myself. My half-sister was a homely and dim-witted girl with the vanity and pride of a much more beautiful and intelligent woman. Despite being a princess, she'd had very few suitors over the years. Although that's as much due to herself as, of course, our mother. Most men feared the princess had inherited the queen's proclivities. Some even wondered if the white bull had been the queen's first indiscretion, as I've often heard whispered through the walls that Ariadne's face was more bovine than mine. It was not. But I can still see their point. She used to come visit me a lot as a child. We would play dice and stones and riddles. But as she grew older, she came to visit less often and always kept her eyes averted, unable to look at me for more than a few moments at a time. I reckoned this was not because she was afraid of me but of any similarities she might see. Eventually, she stopped visiting altogether. I didn't blame her. After all, Mother herself never visited. But I still missed her company… sometimes.

The ugly princess wanted to be a beautiful queen – a queen far away from her controlling father and shameful mother. I couldn't blame her for that either. I only pitied her. She pitied me too. It was the currency we dealt with.

"She's been telling everyone that she loved Theseus before she even met him. That she'd always known she was destined to marry a great man, if not a god," Icarus said.

I rolled my eyes.

"Well, they do say love is blind," the boy quipped.

And yet no one ever loved me, I thought bitterly.

"Power is blind," I told him.

Icarus shrugged. "He is handsome. I'll give him that. Tall, athletic and strikingly good looking, mostly because of his russet hair, so unusual in the Aegean. He's also arrogant, with a wicked smile. But everyone thinks he's charming."

"Not you?"

"No. I can tell charm from cruelty. And arrogance from confidence. He acts as if he's bested you already."

"To celebrate before victory is the privilege of young heroes and old kings. It makes the loss less bitter," I said.

He forced a chuckle, but I could see he was troubled. "What does queen Pasiphae have to say of all this?" I asked, veering the subject.

Icarus swallowed and avoided my gaze. "Not much... She's been pretty melancholic since the news of the bull's death and rarely leaves her rooms. Eros' arrows are... well, they can do a number on a person, even a goddess, it seems."

I had no arguments there. Father always said lust makes monsters of us all. *And what makes monsters, monsters?* I wondered, then took a deep breath and released it in a long, pitiful moan. Neither my mother nor my sister cared for my fate and it was past time to tend my wound. I could feel the blood soaking through the linen bound around my torso, down to my loincloth.

"Well... it is what it is. At least that explains the stampede up there. I guess preparing for a wedding sounds much like preparing for war," I said airily, moving away from grievous thoughts. It was true, though. The walls practically vibrated with human activity. Not just in the upper levels, but in the dungeons as well.

"Hmmm..." Icarus squinted at the ceiling as if he could see through the stone. "The wedding preparations are only part of it. They're looking for someone." He eyed me sheepishly. "I suppose it's probably too late now. Unless..."

I flared my nostrils, too tired to keep prompting the boy.

He cleared his throat. "Have you disposed of the corpses from the last Tribute yet by any chance?"

"No. Why?" The admission caused a pang of embarrassment. I hated leaving dead humans lying around. They stank. Even before they started to decompose.

He smiled enthusiastically. "That's great! They're

still searching for appearance's sake. The Labyrinth is the only place she could have hidden. But no one wants to search in there… which means whatever it is they want from her, you can get it. Father will be pleased."

I closed my eyes and took another deep breath. "Her…?" *The one that got away… It has to be.* Who needs premonition when deduction worked just as well?

"Yes, a woman," Icarus confirmed. "A slave from the west. She used to be a priestess of sorts, or so Father said. Apparently she escaped from the market, infiltrated the palace and took the place of one of the Tributes. How she managed to do that is anyone's guess. She must have been desperate. I mean, sure, no one wants to be a slave. Still, there are worse fates…" He saw my expression and forced a chuckle. "Maybe she wanted to be a hero, eh?"

He, too, thinks I'm a monster, I remember thinking then. Even in Icarus' eyes, that's what I was: a monster and a killer. *A fate worse than slavery, indeed.* I pretended not to have interpreted the meaning of his words and asked, "Why would anyone care about a runaway slave?" After all, if there's one thing Krete had in abundance, it was slaves.

The boy pouted. "I told you: she has something they want. Or she knows something. I'm not sure. Father will tell you more when he comes to see you later. Just… don't throw her body away yet." He stood up. "I need to go before someone misses me. Good luck with the… er… healing." He mimicked my sour expression.

"Don't worry, Father won't let you fight that bastard

at a disadvantage. He's working on a plan." He winked at me. Always so full of hope and optimism, Icarus was.

I waved wearily as he left and all but dragged myself back to the bed. There, I lit a candle with one of Daedalus fire sticks, fetched his special cauterising powder from the medicine chest and got to work.

III

Burning an open wound is as painful as it sounds. I howled like the injured beast that I was. And I must have howled pretty loud because absolute silence followed from above. It's funny how, in order to stop noise, you have make more of it.

I bound the cauterised flesh as best I could with clean linen and, in an effort to overcome the searing ache, took comfort in the fact that at least it no longer bled. I felt so drained, though. So weak. All I wanted to do was sleep. But I reminded myself belligerently, my work was not done yet.

Sleep is just another word for death, Daedalus used to say. He himself rarely slept; always working on something, including ways to stay awake. He believed the soul left the body and became Morpheus' property during sleep. To him, the realms of dream were not much different from the realms of the Underworld. The difference being that Hades, unlike Morpheus, didn't give back our souls.

You find that amusing? I suppose you would. Then again, it doesn't sound like such a bad thing to me. What good is a soul to a corpse? Exactly. Besides, I liked to sleep. I liked to dream too. Dreams were all I had in the Labyrinth – a dangerous possession.

It was in this bleak frame of mind that I set off after the stray female.

Women are different creatures than men. More cautious, cunning, and deceptive. They know they can't win a fight, certainly not one against me. So they run and hide instead. They can be pretty good at it too, since they tend to have stronger survival instincts than men. Their orientation skills, however, are generally worse. They often find themselves at dead ends or treading the same paths over and over again without realising. Not this one, though. I couldn't find any trace of her, nor had I any idea of where she might be.

I grudgingly retraced each step to where I killed the men – all Athenians, judging by their clothes. All fairly fit and well nourished – not common traits amongst slaves or captives. Again, had I been in a more astute state of mind earlier, these details would have raised suspicion.

Athenian Tributes, much like slaves, are far from rare. But an entire group of them? Highly unlikely. These Tributes had been brought by Theseus. I'd bet my tail on it. They were his own group of undesirables: thieves, deserters, dissidents, rivals… basically, chattel acting as scouts for a chance to win back their lives. Their weapons were simple, unornamented but well crafted, sturdy.

This was a prelude, I realised. A test. One I nearly failed.

The women were the same – all attired in garb from the mainland, not the islands. Stars, I felt so stupid then. And annoyed. How could one simple mistake cause so much trouble? It felt as if Fate was laughing at me. Maybe she was…

Anyway… The bodies had set in their death poses, too stiff and awkward to move, which was just as well. I had other priorities. Daedalus always said it was best to finish one task before starting another. A piece of advice he himself never followed, mind, but it didn't make it less wise, I suppose.

I stood there for a while, considering my accursed options. I had no desire to drag stiff corpses into the sewer. Though I'd rather do that than what I had to. Stars, I really didn't want to go chasing after the woman. Even after my disastrous performance, it seemed beneath me, somehow. A horrible thing to think, I know. But I took no pleasure in hunting the helpless, believe it or not. I figured the poor thing must have been terrified, likely curled up, shaking in a corner somewhere. Little did I know…

In any case, I couldn't just wait for her to die, either. I mean, I could. I figured that, left alone, she'd die of thirst in three, maybe four days? But like I already told you, that was not how I liked to do things. Apart from the man I mentioned earlier, I'd only let that happen to one other: a boy who, instead of a weapon, brought a flask of wine into the Labyrinth and offered it to his companions. A last drink, he'd said. The wine was poisoned. They all died in agony while he laughed and laughed. So I let him live a few more days. He'd earned it.

I remember the boy calling for me at the end, begging me to come to him. To kill him. I never did. Didn't pick up his body, either. It's probably still there.

Yes, I suppose I, too, can be cruel under the right circumstances. Still, it wasn't just cruelty that drove me then. I was still curious to find out how long it would take a human to find the centre of the Labyrinth. After all, I'd never really given them the chance to. The boy never found it, though. Neither did the man. They came close many times but always got turned around at the last intersection, for some reason. Daedalus sure knew what he was doing when he designed that maze.

No, I decided. I would not let the poor woman wander in the dark until she died of thirst. I'd have to find her. And kill her. It was hardly a choice. The worst choices are always the ones that have been made for you.

I took a moment to listen. Sniffed at the air. It was hard to pinpoint scents in the midst of so much blood and excreta, so I moved past the corpses until I caught something different, something *warm*. It put me in mind of resin and woodsmoke. Except I couldn't identify the resin and I knew little about wood. It was a sharp scent, somewhat bitter and musky but clean, so different from the other women who covered their odours with oils and perfume. I traced it to the entrance. She'd likely thought she could exit the Labyrinth that way. She couldn't, of course. The door only opened from the outside. Maybe she thought she would wait there and fight her way through the next group of guards. A rational choice. I myself had tried that in my youth. The guards had been prepared for it. They always were. And even *I* couldn't fight my way through a score of veterans, armoured and armed to the teeth.

I resumed my hunt and followed the scent until I stepped on a pile of rough fabric discarded on the floor. It looked like a dress, or what was left of it, purposely torn to shreds. It had to be the woman's, even if the redolent smell of sea water and sun-bathed freedom clinging to the fabric didn't quite match. I cursed. She must have guessed I'd be able to track her by scent, so she'd discarded her clothes. *Clever girl,* I thought with admiration and a fair amount of pity. The clever ones always suffer the most, for they can't help themselves but to try, and if circumstances were different – as in, fair – they would probably survive. Alas, fairness had no place in the Labyrinth. There was only me.

As I told you before, women are technically easier to kill but harder to catch. I suppose they have to be, especially the comely ones. I had no idea if she was comely, mind. I wasn't even sure if she was indeed a she, now that I relive these events with a clear mind. I just figured she had to be. Call it an educated guess – or a wishful fancy. It would explain why she wasn't with the other women, especially if she wasn't part of their group to begin with. Women don't tend to fight amongst themselves to decide who dies first, or pick champions to fight me. Instead, they prefer to single out the fairest or most hated amongst them (women being envious creatures, they tend to go hand in hand) and use her as a sort of sacrifice – or gift – hoping she will appease me or, failing that, distract me.

Much like ugly men like to fuck and kill before being killed, seeing beauty despoiled is the petty satisfaction of ugly women.

But I digress. Beauty was of no consequence down there, in the dark, and all the cleverness in Olympus wouldn't have saved her from me. For there was no salvation, no escape, nowhere to go. And very few places to hide.

The dress had been left as a decoy in an intersection with three possible directions. I took a deep breath, concentrated. And for the life of me, I couldn't decide which way to take. I had not lost her scent. Quite the contrary. It was all around me, as if it wafted off the walls themselves, which made no sense. For an idiotic moment I thought maybe she'd rubbed herself along them, but then a better hypothesis came to mind. I wound up the gyro torch and, sure enough, found bits of fabric neatly placed between the stone. I cursed again. Things were getting interesting all right, but far from easier. Any other day I'd welcome this challenge. That day, though… I growled low in exasperation, then waited, hoping for a despondent sound of her own. No such luck.

Left with few clues and too many options, I decided to take the shortest and most obvious path first. The one that led straight to the exit. It was unlikely I'd find her there – and I didn't – but I had to check. Next I backtracked and took the second option, a path that ran around the outer wall of the Labyrinth for hundreds of yards before it reached a dead end. There were only two possible turns off that corridor: one led straight back to the entrance via a much longer route, the other deep into the heart of the zigzagging maze. The third option was the path I'd taken to get to where I stood, and since I was confident we had not crossed paths and she had not exited the maze, I chose option number two. After all, that was the one I'd pick if I didn't want to be followed – or found.

I advanced slowly. Not only because I was cautious, but as I'd said, I was tired and injured, far from my best self. Under different circumstances, I reckon a part of me would probably have enjoyed the hunt. It'd been so long since anyone had presented a challenge. Right then, though, I could really have done without it. Hunting is only a sport when you do it for pleasure. I felt none.

A few dozen yards on, and I cursed yet again. I'd lost her scent and had no idea which path to take.

That's what you get for being lazy and sloppy, I chastised myself for the umpteenth time. My tail lashed against the walls in frustration. Stars, I was furious. Not the fury of battle but of shame and irritation. I needed rest so I could heal at least well enough to fight a hero. Yet I had to continue searching for a slave girl who'd done me no harm and probably only wanted to live.

There's no rest for the wicked, they say. Or in this case, the stupid. For how was I supposed to rest with her still out there? I shook my head in resignation, picked another path and kept going, growing increasingly nauseous and disgruntled.

The Labyrinth was an elaborate and complex maze of passageways, blank walls, false turns, dead ends and seemingly identical corridors and alcoves, designed for a person to wander in aimlessly for days. I stalked along its passages for hours on end and found nothing, heard nothing, and smelled nothing but the vestiges of the presence of another being. *She must have a superior sense of direction and an uncanny memory to retrace her steps in the dark like that,* I thought. Either that or she could see in the dark. She could be a demigoddess. Or a nymph. They have talents. I'd rather entertain all those notions than admit that I'd been tricked by a girl inside my own domain.

Never underestimate a woman, I reminded myself again and again as I walked until I couldn't think straight with exhaustion, annoyance, boredom, and pain. The wound began bleeding again. I felt lightheaded, unable to concentrate and could hardly pick her scent from the Labyrinth's anymore. She could be anywhere: ten paces ahead or five behind. I had to stop.

It doesn't matter, I assured myself. She wouldn't leave and she wouldn't find the centre, either. And if she died... well, it's the fate of all who entered this place, after all. The only difference was how you died: quickly and violently, or slowly and bitterly. Still, my wounded pride would not let me give up the chase without one last try.

"Enough of this! Show yourself and you won't be harmed." I shouted as loud as I could. No reply came.

"I know you can hear me." In truth, I had no idea if she could hear me or not. My voice carried far, but the Labyrinth was basically one stone wall after another and spread farther still. I just hoped she would listen. Right then, I really did. So I tried again. "I'm not an animal, despite what they say or what you might see. I can talk – *we* can talk and figure this out," I said to the walls. Silence. Yeah, I would not believe my words either. Figure what out, exactly? Her preferred way to die? Stars, at this rate, I'd be dying first.

"Suit yourself," I said to the silence and headed back to my den before I passed out.

I was not prepared for what I found.

"You've got to be kidding me," I said aloud, staring at the empty fruit basket.

My figs were gone. All of them! And the pear and

half a loaf of bread, along with two boiled eggs. Not only that, she'd drunk the wine and taken the bottle – filled with fresh water from the fountain, no doubt. She would not die from dehydration anytime soon. Good for her. Not so much for me. I could have torn my horns out in dismay.

It must have been the middle of the night and the temperature had dropped to a chill. Dungeons were cold, damp places, even in Krete. I took a deep, calming breath, nostrils flaring, and lit the hearth. With all my respect to Daedalus and his inventions, no artificial light can ever replace real flame. I don't know why, but I've always felt soothed by flames. Perhaps it's due to my ancestry or an affinity with the smothered fire within my soul. But whenever I was sad or worried, I would stare into a flame and things wouldn't look so bad after a while – a very long while on this particular occasion.

Once composed, I made sure she wasn't hiding in the room – for I would not put it past the creature at this point – and the iron grid covering the culvert to the sewer was still locked in place (I assumed that meant she might not have been strong enough to lift it – thank the stars), then finally went to bed, thoroughly drained and more than a bit disturbed by this development. I could not believe a human had actually found the path to my den. That changed everything!

My entire life, wretched as it had been, had been lived in relative safety and seclusion. No one had ever reached the centre of the maze. Not a soul. That had been as an immutable law of my subterranean world as the movement of the sun from east to west was to everyone under the open sky. I hadn't even realised how much I relied on that certainty until that moment. Her intrusion made me question not only my safety and competence but the very foundations of my domain. It made me feel vulnerable. Humph, I hadn't understood the meaning of the word up until then, either.

Unable to fall asleep despite my overwhelming tiredness, I got up and put more fuel on the fire, then lit every candle, lantern and oil lamp in the room for good measure. There was no point concealing it now, since she'd already found it. Besides, she might be able to disguise her scent and conceal her steps, but she would still have to cast a shadow, damn her. While I was at it, I also set up every alarm Daedalus had provided me with over the years, such as bells triggered by invisible strings, loose stones set atop pressure points connected to spikes. That sort of thing.

Only once confident she wouldn't catch me off guard as I slept, I could finally rest.

IV

"Are you awake?" Daedalus' voice boomed through the window. "Asterius?" Urgency turned to concern. "Wake up!"

"I'm awake," I said, only just. Pain flared between my ribs when I rolled to the side, sharp enough to make me yelp and bring me to full awareness in an instant. "Yes, I am awake," I repeated, sincerely this time. I looked around with bleary eyes and a murky mind, wondering how long had passed. Everything was as I left it. No trap had been triggered, no food had been touched, and I was still alive, so I deemed it safe to assume the woman had not attempted to enter the den while I slept.

I yawned, then coughed as I crawled the short distance to the wall under Daedalus' critical gaze, too sore and groggy to stand and walk properly. I didn't think I'd slept that long or that deeply but, according to the clock candles, seven hours had passed, and even though I could not explain why, exactly, I had the impression he'd been there for a while.

"The state of you," said Daedalus, a man so lean, worn-out and bedraggled as to be mistaken for a scarecrow. "Icarus told me you'd been injured, but I never imagined..." He finished the sentence with a shake of his head. The disappointment behind his concern cut deep.

"I'm sorry, Father. I… failed." My head tilted forward, heavy with the admission.

He dismissed my apologies and gestured to the bloody linen coming undone around my ribs. "Let me see that."

I peeled off the bandage and pressed my side against the narrow opening for him to get a better look. Several imprecations followed.

"What sort of weapon did this?"

"A dagger. The bastard twisted it," I said.

More imprecations. "Did you clean the wound?"

"Yes. With your strongest ointment and fire."

He clicked his tongue. "And a poor job you did of it, I see. You should have waited for me."

"I didn't know when you were coming and I had to stop the bleeding somehow," I protested.

The hard disapproval grumbled under his breath, mixed with the clatter of metal as he rummaged through his satchel, selecting tools I could not name.

"Stand up closer to the wall, please. Hold on to something and try to remain still while I fix this," he commanded dispassionately. To Daedalus, flesh was just another material, like iron, wood or clay, to be worked on and with.

I collapsed back to the floor after his long and excruciating ministrations, mercilessly and awkwardly applied through the narrow window, then bound the wound again according to his instructions, my hands shaking.

"There. That should keep it closed. Now drink this

to stop the rot." He presented me with something that looked and smelled much like how I imagined rotten Ambrosia would. It was the foulest potion I'd ever tasted, but I managed to keep it down.

"Now. Tell me what happened," he said. "Leave nothing out. Remember: the truth is in the details."

Through a haze of pain and intoxication, I went through the events of the previous day as accurately and succinctly as I could under the circumstances, leaving no room for misinterpretation, idealisation, or excuse for my failure.

"So the woman is still alive. Good."

"Why is that good?" The question sounded more hostile than I intended. I didn't wish her harm, mind, only to understand what made her so important to him.

"She has something I want," Daedalus said rather circumspectly.

"What?"

"Information."

"About…?"

He bristled. "That's what I want to know! If they want it, it must be important. I must have it first." There was a feverish edge behind his words.

"Who's they?"

He hesitated before answering, realising he'd said more than he'd intended to. "The gods."

"Gods?" I echoed, for I had not expected that answer. "Which gods?"

"That is irrelevant. Gods are all the same. The Universe's gravest mistake, every single one of them."

Hey! His words, not mine.

"You will find her and bring her here, to me," he said. "I want her alive and able to speak, at least. Now, clearly you're not at your best. And, understandably, you have a soft spot for the gentler sex, but you must remember your duty."

"I never forget it," I said dryly, offended that he equated my failure to forgetfulness and fairly outraged at the implication that such failure had to do with softness of any kind.

"Who is she?" I asked, hoping to learn something I could use to my advantage.

"I believe she's a priestess the barbaric Underworld worshippers of the west sent as Tribute – a poisoned gift." Daedalus shook his head. "I keep telling Minos not to accept Tributes from that peninsula or any other shore beyond the pillars of Heracles. Nothing good ever came from the ocean, I tell you." It was another one of Daedalus' sayings. I wondered if he ever realised that, in a way, I too came from the ocean.

"A priestess from the west…" I mused. "Are you sure?"

He frowned. "Why do you question my word?"

I felt the heat of his discerning gaze on me. Daedalus did not need to light up his eyes with flames to burn you on the spot with a look. Believe me.

"It's only that the other Tributes – all of them – were dressed as Athenians," I explained.

"Have you been stabbed in the brain, Asterius? Perhaps you lost too much blood to reason properly. Didn't Icarus tell you the woman killed the Athenian Tribute and took her place? Garments are part of a person's identity. So obviously she took those as well." The frown deepened into a shrewd squint. "I can see you've developed a sort of admiration for the creature. Don't. Remember what I told you about women: A woman's power lies in –"

"– in being underestimated by men, yes, I know," I said, irritated, because he was right. That had been exactly why I'd lost her. I had forgotten – or ignored – that piece of wisdom.

The reminder was as much for Daedalus' benefit as mine, though. He was the one who'd underestimated my mother. Long before Poseidon had sent the white bull to Krete, Pasiphae had tried to seduce Daedalus. When he'd refused her, she'd had his wife thrown from a cliff. No one had been able to prove this, of course. Such deaths are always deemed accidental or self-inflicted, but many a time I heard the walls whisper that the queen would never suffer a woman more beautiful than she in the palace.

They say men are beasts. That might be so. But a jealous woman is the cruelest thing in the universe. Take Medea, for example, Hera or even Athena. As Zeus once said, a dried-up cunt is a sign of a shrivelled heart and a venomous soul. He should know.

"Women are dangerous, devious, vicious creatures. This one especially. She's resourceful. Perhaps not entirely human," Daedalus warned. He, much like his perpetual motion engines, had a way of carrying on a conversation by himself.

"Yes, I figured as much." I sighed.

"She didn't just infiltrate the Tributes in a desperate attempt to escape slavery. She killed one of the women.

Broke her neck clean and hid the body down a latrine shaft. This suggests she wasn't trying to escape the palace. She wanted to be here, in the Labyrinth, on purpose. That worries me."

It also suggests she has to be pretty strong for a woman and skilled in killing, I thought, but held my tongue. "Can she be working for Theseus, you think?" I asked instead.

Daedalus pondered this with furtive eyes. "Unlikely. Although you know how I feel about coincidence."

"'Coincidence is the name Fate uses when she wishes to remain anonymous'," I quoted. "Right... don't worry, Father. I'll deal with her as I've dealt with all who have been sent here." *And the less I know about her or her motives, the easier it will be,* I decided, for however reluctantly or misguidedly, I had indeed developed a sort of admiration, even respect for the resourceful priestess.

"Make sure you do," Daedalus said sternly.

"Yes, Father," I reassured him, eager to move the subject from my past failure to my future problem. "What about this Theseus?" I asked. "Aren't you worried about him?"

Daedalus puffed out an exasperated breath. "He's just another ambitious boy with a large ego. Heroes are all the same: Predictable. Basic. Greedy. Vain."

"He did kill the white bull," I pointed out.

"And now he thinks he can kill you too! But you're not a brainless bull, are you? And this is not an empty field. You have the advantage. You know the layout, you have the weapons, the strength *and* the skill to kill him if you keep your wits about you."

"What do you mean?"

"He's the sort of hero who likes to talk, to tease and

taunt his victims. Don't let him cloud your reasoning with honeyed words and you'll succeed over him."

I nodded. "And when can I expect this success?"

"The wedding is not for a few days yet. Ariadne wants a big event. I've encouraged it. I told Minos that to rush or hush the affair would make people suspect the princess was with child. The last thing the king wants is more scandalous speculations involving bastards. It's bought us some time. Even if all this brainless activity around fabrics and flower arrangements drains my patience and hinders my creativity." He rolled his eyes. "I swear, shallowness of intellect is contagious."

"Let Ariadne have her moment, Father. The gods know she probably won't have many." Despite circumstances, I still thought of Ariadne as my big sister and wanted the best for her.

"I didn't do it for her sake," he assured me. "The wedding would have been yesterday if Theseus had his way. The boy seems more eager to spend his nuptials here than with his bride."

"Humph," I said. Not knowing what else to say to that.

Daedalus fell silent for a moment. His dark, sunken gaze fixed on me in a way that made me feel like a tool about to be used, rather than a person. He was always analytical and often critical. His stare inscrutable and uncomfortable. But right then I felt there was something else in his mind: a vague speculation uncharacteristic of the man.

"Father?" I waited for him to meet my eyes. "What aren't you telling me?"

Daedalus had made a vow never to lie. Some said it

was the price he'd paid for his genius, part of a bargain with the trickster Titan Prometheus. Others, a curse from the god Hephaestus for rivalling his talents. He never revealed which. And just because he couldn't lie, nothing stopped him from withholding the truth.

"I've told you all you need to know," said he.

"Shouldn't I be the judge of that? After all, I'm the one who has to fight the damned hero. I want the truth, Father."

"Some truths are complicated." He shook his head, brow furrowing. "No, that's not fair. You're bright enough for complicated." He pressed his lips, arguing with himself about how to proceed. "The fact of the matter is, truth can be a lot like prophecy. When you believe something is true, you make it so. Does that make sense? Sometimes it's better to remain ignorant and keep an open mind. Find out your own truth."

The answer was quite unsatisfactory and out of character, but I trusted his judgement and did not insist. I wish I had.

"I'll leave you alone now, so you can heal," he said in the same uncharacteristically gentle tone. "You'll need all your strength for this one. Theseus has been locked in his quarters with his best men, training day and night to fight you. He'll be prepared. But he's no match for you." He smiled and his pride in me felt like how I imagined sunlight to be. "I'll return tomorrow evening with more supplies. That should give you enough time to find and subdue the female, yes?" A command rather than a question. I felt cold again, in the shadow.

"I hope so," I mumbled, not enthused, but confident I would accomplish the task. "Once I have her, what should I ask her? What sort of information are you looking for, Father?" I asked in case something went wrong, like for example, I accidentally killed the creature instead of catching her. It could happen.

Daedalus frowned, considering his answer, then after a fair amount of lip licking and tongue clicking, he said, "Anything about souls, gods or the Underworld."

"The Underworld?!" *Who the fuck cares about the Underworld?* I almost spat, but I could tell by his stern and haunted gaze that he clearly did.

"Yes, Asterius," he replied tiredly. "The gods are up to something. I can sense it. But I can't guess at it beyond a suspicion it has something to do with souls in the Underworld."

Again, I wondered why he would care. The Labyrinth might have been Underworld-adjacent, but I knew very little about it or the gods who ruled it. And of souls, well… I knew even less. I'd often wondered if I had a soul. I figured I must have. I am the grandson of a Titan, after all. They're known to have had the most powerful souls. If only I knew what to do with it, though. Souls are what power Will, but my will had no power of its own.

Daedalus had always said humans, although gifted with souls and free will, lacked the mind and discipline to wield them the way gods do. He always sounded as if he didn't consider himself human. Maybe he didn't. And my will, now that I think about it, had always been his. No more than the will of a weapon, a thing. As in, none at all. I was an object, and objects are always subject to another's will.

Then something occurred to me.

"Do you think this woman might be a daemon or something?" I asked, concerned. Daemons were beings whose nature was neither mortal nor divine. Their souls able to cross realms beyond even those of life and death. I had no idea how to fight those things, let alone catch one.

"No, nothing of the sort," he assured me. "She's more an agent than a daemon, I reckon. Regardless, we need to know what – or who – we're dealing with." He stood up to leave. "If I can't come by tomorrow for some reason, I'll send Icarus instead. Tell him whatever you learn from her. I trust you'll have made her talk by then."

I nodded. Hoping it was true. Then frowned, unwilling to accept the meaning concealed by his reasonable tone. But it was there, as clear as his words could never be. He, much like Icarus, saw me as a monster capable of forcing confessions out of mortals through sheer terror. The realisation made my heart sink and my fists clench.

A tool, a beast, a monster. That's all I was. Even in the mind of the brightest man that ever lived. The man I called Father. My mentor and protector. The man who'd taught me everything I knew. And also the man responsible for all the things I did not know.

Yes, I'd terrified and killed many. I hadn't wanted to. But I'd had to. And it got easier as I got better at it. I told you before that I was bored with it. And the truth is, I've never felt guilt or regret for my kills. Never felt sorry for those I killed, either. I only really felt sorry for myself. And I wondered then, as I had done many times before, if maybe I had become the monster everyone claimed and that was why even Daedalus and Icarus saw me as one.

'Monsters are made, not born,' Daedalus used to tell me as a child to comfort me. But what difference did that make? To humans, a monster is a monster is a monster. And that's that.

Tears of sorrow and rage welled in my eyes but remained unshed. "Yes, *Father*," I said, without looking at him.

He left.

And for the first time in my life, I was not sorry to see him go.

V

Whatever foul concoction Daedalus had given me seemed to work. The pain subsided considerably and I started feeling better overall shortly after he'd left – physically, at least. Emotionally, I remained wrecked. Still, my appetite had returned, along with my physical strength and stamina. Once fed and invigorated, I set out after the troublesome Tribute. The last thing I needed when the *hero*, Theseus, came with his friends to kill me was another enemy hidden in the maze, ready to stab me in the back.

I left the fire burning in the hearth (I figured if she'd found it once in the dark, she'd find it again with or without light). Then, with my favourite battle axe in hand and Daedalus' lantern charged and ready, I headed straight towards the entrance.

As before, her scent seemed to be everywhere and nowhere. I couldn't track it properly but I could to some degree eliminate the areas she hadn't been yet, which comprised, I realised with mixed feelings, most of the maze.

As far as I could tell, she'd never once deviated from the correct path, as if she'd known the layout beforehand. That had to be impossible, of course, and yet my senses told me otherwise... *Maybe she got lucky*, was my first thought. *Lucky enough to pick the correct route all the way from the entrance to the dome?* Another thought immediately countered. *No one's that lucky*, I decided. Maybe she'd been gifted with extraordinary memory, able to recall each corridor and turn accurately: a more reasonable explanation. Except neither Tyche nor Mnemosyne were particularly generous with their gifts. Quite the contrary.

I don't like this, I kept thinking with increasing frequency as I patrolled the length of the main path of the maze, back and forth like a blind ox. Finally, I'd had enough. I would not play the game by her rules. After all, if we were playing cat and mouse, I had to be the cat.

I put the search on hold and attended to the dead bodies. They'd started to stink, bloat and ooze foul fluids. I had to dispose of them. Under normal circumstances, this was not a laborious task. I'd just drag the carcasses by the ankle, two, sometimes three at a time, dumped them down the waste shaft and be done with it. But my side still ached, so I dragged the corpses one by one, taking care not to open or aggravate the cursed wound, which of course I ended up doing anyway, when I lifted the heavy iron grid to the sewer.

I've often wondered if the bodies ended up washed up on some shore or caught in a fisherman's net. Or if maybe they simply piled up outside the palace walls. Likely all three. At least for some of them. But if that were the case, why would people still believe I ate them? Weak-minded people will always believe whatever they choose to, regardless of the evidence. And the strong minded, well, they don't believe in anything except everyone else's stupidity. Prometheus giving creative fire to humans was as useless as a pig herder giving pearls to his swine, in my opinion, and he sure paid the price for it. We all still do.

Ah, you laugh and shake your head but I can tell you agree. And I bet people believe all sorts of lies and misconceptions about you, too. It's the price of not being ordinary.

Anyway, that miserable task took me the best part of the day. It was a big maze. Yes, I know I keep saying it, but I'm not sure I'm getting across just how vast it really was. The Labyrinth spread beneath not only the palace of Knossos but the city itself, all the way down to the coast, taking advantage of the liminal realms that composed the natural maze of caves where Zeus was born. Legend said some of these caves led to the Underworld and other places where reality was less, well... real. Sometimes I could swear I heard as many voices from below as from above. But I'd never given it much thought, to be honest. Not until Daedalus brought up the Underworld that day. He himself had often dismissed the idea as nonsense and superstition. "The Underworld is not even underground," he'd told me once, "but a world in and of itself, a realm existing alongside the one we perceive as reality."

"That would explain my situation," I'd replied in jest, rather inclined to believe in superstition than in his rational explanation. The very idea of the Underworld spilling into the maze was not a pleasant one. I found it disturbing, not to mention sad, to think the living and the dead existed practically side by side and yet might as well be across galaxies from each other. Now I wonder if the truth lies somewhere in between, like a limbo between realms. After all, I've walked every path in the maze and met no dead I had not killed myself. But the voices I'd heard… those were not just my imagination, were they?

All right! There's no need to get flammable. Tell the story first, ask questions later. Got it. Moving on.

I finally got to the body of the man who'd stabbed me. Petty distaste had made me save him for last. And I was punished for it. He stunk worse than rotten fish by that point. Once again, I wondered about Daedalus' rationalisations about death and souls. He once told me about a god of the Underworld from the lands south of Krete that would preserve bodies after death long enough for the soul to return if it wished to – mummies, they called them. I always thought that to be cruel. Why not create a new body? If I were a god of the dead, I'd rather put souls in formidable, near indestructible bodies, not desiccated corpses. I told him as much. He laughed at the idea. It was one of the few times I actually saw him laugh. Then he got that glint in his eyes that always meant he'd had an idea and left without so much as a farewell, so absorbed he was in it.

What's wrong? No, I have no idea what he did afterwards. We never talked about it again. And yes, clearly I know very little about being a god, as you say.

Back to the story. As I bent to pick up the man by his foot, I felt, rather than heard, something behind me. That distinct and eerie feeling of being watched gave me pause. Feigning nonchalance as best I could, I cast around the darkness and thought I glimpsed something: an eye. A single yellow eye, inhumanly large and close to the floor, boring into mine.

It was pitch dark. The lantern had just gone out, so it couldn't have been a reflection or distant glow caused by it. Which only left my imagination. Daedalus' potions sometimes played tricks with the mind, so I didn't make much of it at first. I shook my head to clear it and wound up the gyro torch. Light flooded the corridor again. I was alone with the corpse. Not far from us lay the dagger, barely six inches long, the blade stained by time and scratched with use, but still sharp. It had a small piece of ember embedded in the handle. The handle itself was made of a wood I could not identify: odd to the touch and striated like muscle, decorated with spirals carved on one side and an Ouroboros on the other. I'd never seen one like it. But I had seen better.

Before I continue, it's worth saying there was nothing special about the man who'd stabbed me. I stared at his face – or what was left of it – and I couldn't help feeling sick at the thought that if this human, this mortal being, this pile of rotting flesh and broken bone, had almost killed me with such a puny weapon, what chance did I have against a hero? How had I become so complacent, careless and jaded – so… weak? Right then, I almost wished I was dead. I believed I deserved to be dead.

Stars, if only I'd had a potion to heal my mood and poor judgement that day. A dull mind can be as foul as the decaying flesh of a corpse. And far more debilitating.

I hadn't even realised how much I'd been procrastinating, standing there brooding. How proactive I'd been in avoiding the hunt. The truth was, I'd rather have dealt with all the dead and the rotting than face another living being right then…

After I dumped the body down the shaft, I spared another look at the dagger, threw it on the bed, then returned to the scene of the slaughter with a bag of sand to cover up the mess. Again, I could swear I was being watched as I worked. I spun around, and this time, I definitely glimpsed that *yellow eye*, for lack of a better description.

Now, when I said I could see in the dark, I might have exaggerated a bit. My eyes were well accustomed to the dark, true, and perhaps because of the Titan blood in me, I could sometimes discern shapes and even movement in the darkest gloom. But it was more due to an instinct than actual sight. I don't have what the gods call Reach and I can't actually *see* details or colours without light. Still, I definitely saw something – or someone – just as the light flared behind the glass of the gyro torch to reveal an empty corridor.

I cursed inwardly and went back to spreading the sand, my eyes fixed on the ground but my ears perked, searching for any sound. That's when I noticed a length of string running along the base of the wall. At first I figured it must have been ripped from a garment during a fight, unravelled after being caught on the rough edge of a stone or something. But upon closer inspection, this string had never been woven into fabric. It was both strong and soft, expertly spun and dyed similar in colour to the stone. I plucked at it, discovering it led into the darkness, so I followed it along the long corridor, guided by curiosity and a sinking feeling in my stomach.

I knew exactly where it would lead, long before I got there.

The thread disappeared through the narrow slit between the stone floor and the heavy door at the exit. The door itself was locked, as usual, but someone had secured the string somewhere behind it before it closed. I ripped it free and began winding it up into a ball. Once I had a handful of it, I could clearly discern the pungent scent of lavender and rose water – Ariadne's scent. But there were other scents hidden behind those: not floral, not feminine at all, in fact. The smell of iron, sweat and garlic. I wrinkled my nose in distaste and kept gathering the thread. As you can guess, it lead straight back to the hearth.

It was well into the night by then. The palace was finally quiet – or as quiet as a palace housing hundreds of servants preparing for a royal wedding can be. That uncanny feeling of being watched raised the hairs on my nape and tickled my ears as I walked, wherever I walked. Try as I might, I could not shake it off, just as I could not ignore the impossible glimpse of a cat's eye in the darkness now and again.

I was about two-thirds of the way back, walking along one of the longest stretches of the maze, when I sensed a sort of draft against the back of my calves, a displacement in the air. I did not slow down, my pace already deliberately slow, but I remained highly alert.

That was, I realised, a great place for an ambush. There were only two other ways out of that corridor: one on each side of the passage, and both led to dead ends. An idea took shape in my mind.

I turned without breaking stride, took two paces and felt that displaced air again. Her scent was all around me. I lashed out with my tail, hitting flesh. A rather unfeminine yelp of pain and surprise followed, then panicked shuffling. I tracked the sound. Caught off guard and hoping to elude me as soon as possible, she turned into the nearest dead end. I felt triumphant and slightly vindicated, for I'd finally understood her strategy. All this time, she'd been playing with me. She could have hidden anywhere and waited, but the only place she was truly safe was the one where I'd already looked. The place I'd just left. And so she'd been following me; the gods know for how long. That's why I couldn't track her scent properly. She'd been behind me the entire time! *This girl has balls*, I thought. But now I finally had her and what a shame it would be to kill her…

I heard her anxious breathing, heard her palms frantically patting the walls. I could almost hear her thinking, desperate to find a solution, an escape. She knew she'd made a mistake. Knew she was trapped. I had blocked the tunnel with my double-sided battle axe and my bulk.

Yes, some would say such an axe was too big to wield in a narrow space. Well, I, too, am too big for most spaces. Besides, it wasn't *that* narrow, and I needed a weapon able to not only block my opponents but to keep them at a distance as well. Not to mention, the sight of it was often enough to dissuade an attack in the first place. And, more to the point, I like big axes.

Confident she couldn't get past me, I wound up the lantern. Light flooded the corridor. And I saw not her, but... *him.*

"Well done. You finally got me," he said.

Such was my stupefaction, I failed to notice the triggerbow aimed at my head until it was too late.

It all went dark.

VI

I woke up on the stone floor, unarmed, with a monstrous headache. My skull hurt horrours too, and the lump on my forehead felt like another horn trying to burst through the skin.

"Fuck," I croaked in the dark, taking stock of myself and my surroundings. Being dead seemed unlikely, considering the amount of pain I was in and I was still inside the Labyrinth. Definitely not alone, though.

"Good, you're awake," came a man's voice. I bolted upright to face the speaker. The sudden movement aggravated my stab wound and headache in equal amounts. I had to brace myself against the wall, struggling to remain upright. Through the ringing in my ears I heard the turn of the flywheel, and the blurry image of the speaker became clear.

Theseus sat across from me in the corridor, eating the last of my figs. I knew it to be him by the russet hair and the handsome face set in that insufferable expression of confidence and defiance common to men used to getting their way. He was completely naked in the fashion of both heroes and beasts, displaying an impressive amount of scars crisscrossing an almost superhuman physique. His eyes were covered by an oblong lens, fastened round his head by a leather band -- the yellow eye, I realised. He took it off to reveal an intelligent gaze, put the torch down next to the ball of yarn and casually aimed the triggerbow – one of Daedalus' deadliest inventions – at me. The loaded bolt was sharp-tipped this time, not blunt.

How long have I been out? I wondered, although it really made no difference. I'd been beaten. Taken down without even putting up a fight. If shame could kill…. Then it hit me. Why was I still alive? If the sadistic hero thought to catch me instead and parade me in chains through the streets of Athens to aggrandise his ego, he was sorely mistaken. I restrained myself from charging him. It wouldn't do to be put down like a rabid beast either. I decided to bide my time, to wait for the right moment, to make the most of being alive and survive this turn of events. *Easier thought than done…*

"Honoured to meet you, daemon," Theseus said.

He's still mocking me, I thought. "How did you get in here?" I asked. A dumb question. After all, there was only one entrance. Both Icarus and Daedalus had said he would not fight me until after he married Ariadne. But then I remembered Daedalus also said that he had been locked away, out of sight, *training. Right.* Still, he would not have been able to elude, or even bribe, all the guards to gain entrance. And Minos would never let him anywhere near the Labyrinth until he'd secured his claim to Athens through Ariadne's hand. Which left only one option.

"I killed a witch and took her place in the last group of Tributes," Theseus said matter-of-factly. "Ariadne told me you avoid killing women, and I always wanted to wear a dress," he added glibly. "Funny, by the way she spoke, I expected to find you here with a harem. My men will be so disappointed."

"You –" I hesitated. My head hurt so much it was painful to speak. "*You* killed the Tribute?"

"No. I killed a priestess. She killed the Tribute. Although I cannot fathom why she'd been so keen to come here that she couldn't wait her turn." He pretended to consider this. "Maybe she had the gift of foresight and knew I would kill you first. The funny thing is, catching her killing the slave was what gave me the idea to come unannounced, shall we say."

"And the gear?" I asked.

"The thread was given to me. The eye and bow I took from her. And we both know where she'd got them, don't we?"

Yes, I knew Daedalus hadn't told me everything. I even speculated that his motives for having me chase this mystery woman were more personal and mundane than he'd led me to believe. Maybe she'd stolen from him. Tricked him, somehow. That might explain why he'd acted so sheepishly and antagonist towards the woman. But why would he make up a story about information and gods and bring the Underworld into it? Was he testing me? It made no sense, though. How would she even gain access to his workshop or to the palace itself? Was she a bed slave, perhaps? Would he hide that from me? *Probably*, I conceded. Daedalus was a proud man. He would never admit bedding a slave, never mind a priestess. Not even to me. Still… something did not add up.

I rubbed my forehead, feeling dizzy again. "Why

would Daedalus want me to kill her, then?" I wondered aloud.

"Correct me if I'm wrong, but as I overheard it, he wanted you to find her, not kill her. My guess is that this" – he waved the triggerbow – "was meant for you, to use on me. It's a bit too big to fit through the window, no?"

I tried to remember what Daedalus had said about prophecy and truth. If he'd wanted me to have the bow, he'd have designed one that fit through the opening or figured out another way of giving it to me, like he did with everything else, including weapons. No, the triggerbow must have been for her own protection. He wanted me to find her, to learn something from her he could not tell me himself. But he had not accounted for Theseus' interference, and now…

"What a remarkable piece of engineering, isn't it?" said he, still admiring the bow. "Imagine having an army equipped with these. It would conquer the world."

"What did you do with my axe?"

He looked annoyed at being so rudely interrupted. "Somewhere safe, out of your reach. That thing could split me in two!"

"I don't need an axe for that," I boasted.

He laughed. "But it would take a lot more effort, wouldn't it?"

I growled. "What do you want?"

"Why, to kill you."

"Then why haven't you done so already?"

He feigned offence. "You were unconscious. Where's the fun in that?"

"You think killing is fun?" I sneered.

"Very much so! I was born to kill. It's what I'm good at. Might as well enjoy it. Don't you?"

"No."

"Liar."

"Fuck you."

I charged him, head down, ready to impale him on my horns. He got to his feet, and he aimed the trigger-bow at my head in earnest, a stern warning on his face. I stopped.

For a moment we just stood there, gazes locked in a contest of wills – how long I cannot say. Time, never particularly relevant inside the Labyrinth, seemed to have been left out of this meeting altogether. All I remember is the moment itself. Sometimes I remember it as a fleeting moment. Others, it feels like forever. Memory is funny that way.

However long it lasted, it eventually ended when he raised an appeasing hand. I didn't react. Didn't move. Or speak. But my eyes left his to look at the hand. And just like that, the moment ended.

"I'm awake now, so you better kill me – *hero*. For you know, I cannot let you live either."

He laughed again. The sound grated in my ears, scraping through my mind straight to my soul.

"How tragic we are," he said ruefully. "Yes, we'll fight and one of us will die. It is our fate. But I'd rather kill time first, if you don't mind."

"Huh?"

He gestured with the bow for me to sit back down. "Let's talk for a while."

"You want to *talk*?"

"Why the surprise? We're talking right now, aren't we? Pretty much every monstrous beast I've slayed has been just that, a beast. Mindless and mute. You seem to have a mind of your own and the ability to articulate your thoughts better than a priestess of Athena. So yes, I'd very much like to keep talking with you before I kill you. If nothing else, it will give you time to recover. I mean, look at you! You can hardly stand. I'm here to fight you, not to put you down like a lame horse." There was that insufferable grin again. "So, once again, I suggest we talk, man to man, not hero to monster. Let's ignore for the moment that we're mortal enemies. Or are you so desperate to die? If that's the case, I'll gladly oblige you. But… hear me out. I'm not offering you a truce out of the kindness in my heart, not even out of sportsmanship or pride – there's that, yes – but mostly, I'm offering you a truce because I was brought here to kill a beast and I don't like being lied to and used as a tool by men unable to do the deed themselves. That being said, and if you prefer, I will kill you where you stand."

He stared at me dispassionately, and I saw what Icarus meant when he'd said he was soulless. His eyes were dark and captivating like the Styx. His gaze laden with cunning and greed: greed for knowledge, power and, above all, life. For he was dead inside. But with a face like that, no one could see it but me. For I, too, hungered for the same things.

"Please," he added with a solicitous gesture. I'm pretty sure I gaped at him then.

My head still ached, and I knew as long as I saw two Theseus instead of one, I could not fight him and win. But I had no patience for wordplay or mind games either. My first impulse was to lash out, tell him to fuck off again and let Fate decide. Even shot in the head, I'd have a good chance of crushing him with my dead weight, if nothing else. *Patience,* I told myself, reluctant to stoop to such desperate tactics. *Keep your wits about you,* Daedalus had said. I drew a deep breath. Then another.

"All right," I said civilly. "Let's talk. But not here. I'm hungry and thirsty and this cursed wound needs tending. I'm going back to my room. You're welcome to follow." I walked towards him. He moved out of the way to let me pass, and I kept walking, confident he would not pull the trigger. Now I wish he had. Perhaps then you and I wouldn't be having this conversation.

"After you," he said mockingly, behind my back.

By the time I had enough presence of mind to even think about turning around, disarm him and smash his smile to pieces, he had already dropped too far behind, still casually but unerringly aiming the bow at my head. A monster should not have thought twice about it. But how could I kill a man who'd just passed on another opportunity to kill me?

No, it wasn't honour. That's the motivation poets assign heroes to make them seem more virtuous than the common man, and in doing so, justify their deeds. I had no honour to speak of. It was curiosity that stopped me, nothing more. Daedalus once told me that in the ancient kingdom to the south of Krete, the gods took on the aspect of cats and that curiosity was the only thing that could kill them. I guess I played the role of the cat in this chase far better than I should have.

Seriously, it wasn't that funny. Why are you still laughing? Right, then…

We strolled in silence for most of the way, with nothing but our breathing, the hushed rustling of movement and the occasional grind of the lantern wheel to disturb it. I found myself welcoming the harsh sound of the gyro, for never before had silence been so uncomfortable to my ears. Always accustomed to it, even longing for it, I had now learned the huge difference between the silence of solitude and the silence of suspense. And I did not care for the latter.

"You came alone," I said to break the silence. "I did not expect that."

"I'm a hero," he replied, and there was definitely bitterness in his tone. The statement itself spoke volumes.

Slowly, my sluggish mind began to overcome my wounded pride, and I began to understand how I'd misjudged this hero. Of course he would not share the glory with his companions. He would want all the glory for himself, alone. And let's not forget, he liked to play with his victims, to taunt them before he killed them. I would not make it easy or fun for him to slay me, for I, too, could fight with wit, long enough for his guard to falter at least. Then I'd put an end to the conversation with my fist.

"But you cheated," I said.

I heard his pace falter slightly, but his voice remained steady, his tone nonchalant. "How so?"

"You took a slave's rightful place in the Tribute, and instead of fighting alongside them, you hid. You cheated your way through the maze with that yarn and the eye that allows you to see in the dark. Those actions can't really be called heroic, now, can they?"

He stopped, and I turned to face him. The torch had nearly gone out, leaving just enough light to read the animosity between us.

"Ariadne warned me your tongue was harsher than your looks."

"Did she? It doesn't take much to abrade her feelings, tender as they are. Does she know you're here? I thought you were supposed to make her your bride before turning her into a widow."

He squinted at me, not taking the bait. There was something besides annoyance in that squint, a hint of both amusement and revulsion. And something more, something that I could not name then, but I know now to have been foresight.

"Ariadne will be my bride, but she'll never be my wife," said he.

I snorted. "Then you'd better tell her that. She thinks she has you wrapped around her fingers like that piece of string in your hand. Let me guess, a wedding gift?" I felt that piercing pang of betrayal in my chest, almost as sharp as the one between my ribs. I coughed. The taste of blood filled my mouth. I spat it out.

"What can I say? The girl is in love – with herself mostly, as much as the idea of marrying me. Still, I have to give it to her. It's quite a clever idea. Without the yarn, I'd have been lost, even able to see my way in the dark."

I'm not sure she's the one you have to thank, I mused. It made sense that she'd been the one who taught him how to navigate the maze, but such an elegant solution had to have come from a brighter and far more practical mind. She might have spun the thread and given it to him but I doubted she'd know how to use it like this.

My guess was that the yarn had been meant for the priestess along with the rest of his gear.

"What did you do with the priestess's body?" I asked him offhandedly.

"Gave it to my men. I figured while everyone was looking for her, they wouldn't be looking for me."

"Humph." *He will not kill me*, I remember thinking as I turned around again and resumed our march. It was more a feeling than a thought. A sort of premonition, almost. He would not kill me because I was already dead. So was he. All who enter the Labyrinth are dead, with or without a thread.

The hearth of the Labyrinth lay just around the corner. I stopped short of the entrance and stepped aside to let him pass. "Guests first," I told him insincerely, smiled and braced myself to take him down.

He raised an eyebrow at me and managed a pout as he smiled back. "I'm a hero. Not a fool. If this truce, or whatever you want to call it, is going to work, we need to trust each other for as long as it lasts. I could have killed you a dozen times in the last twenty-four hours. Extend me the same courtesy for the rest of this day so we can have a conversation like civilised men."

"Is that what we are?" My nostrils flared. I had no mind to be mocked and, for a moment, saw myself reaching for his neck just to prove my point.

He saw my intention and took a step back, pointedly not aiming the bow. "Peace, brother. I'm not laughing at you, but with you. We're both past civilisation. Although, I have to admit" – he glanced at the shelves where dozens of scrolls lay neatly arranged – "you've more wisdom inside these walls than King Minos' and

Aegeus' combined libraries. If knowledge was power, one could rule the Aegean from here. I envy your collection and the time you've had to read it. But, alas, heroes can't be scholars. The gods prefer us stupid, obedient and impulsive. I reckon you're none of those things."

"No, I'm no hero," I said scornfully. "Very well, give me your weapon and go sit on that chair," I told him.

"Give me your word that you won't try anything stupid."

"My word?" No one ever cared about such a thing. The fact that he did made me want to scream.

"Yes. We are nothing without our word," he said in earnest.

I only nodded, grinding my teeth but unable to disagree.

He puckered his lips, in what I figured was an attempt not to smile, then placed the yarn, the lantern and the bow on the table deliberately, one by one, and ambled over to the fountain. There he cupped his hands in the basin and drank deeply before splashing water over his face. I watched this standing still in stunned silence. For what sort of monster would I be had I done otherwise?

"You keep a very clean den for a beast," Theseus said, glancing at me over his shoulder, making sure I remained true to my word, under the pretence of taking in the room. "The whole maze, actually. Very tidy."

"Did you expect me to walk around in filth, crushing bones beneath my hooves?"

He considered this, amused. "Yes, actually. But I'm glad to be wrong."

He cupped the fresh water again and bent over the basin, nearly plunging his whole face in it. Would have been so easy to kill him then, to drown him there, and throw him down the sewer like the others. These thoughts had to be forced, though. In truth, I had no desire to do that. Sure, I knew I would have to kill him eventually, and the longer I waited, the longer we talked, the harder that task would be. *Might as well get it over with.*

He glanced around sharply, eyes narrowing in my direction as if he'd heard my thoughts. I froze. He finished his ablutions and moved to stand in front of the dying hearth embers, hands stretched out to dry. The gesture implied more habit than discomfort. Then he grabbed a piece of cheese from the basket and finally sank onto my favourite chair – not the one I told him to – looking at me obstinately.

"By all means, make yourself at home. Eat something, why don't you – just as you did before," I said waspishly. Whatever else Theseus was, he sure was bold. But I'd not fall for such childish tactics.

I'd lost track of time again, but as far as I could tell by instinct and the activity above, I'd wasted the entire night with this chase. No wonder I was exhausted and way overdue in changing the bandages. I sat on the bed and opened the medicine chest.

"So, where shall we start?" he asked.

"You're the one who wants a conversation, so you choose while I change this. Fair warning, make any attempt to retrieve the bow and –" I blinked at the walls. The place was filled with weapons. Spears, maces, knives, and even swords lay within his reach. "Touch any weapon and the conversation is over," I rephrased severely.

He nodded, then whistled at the sight of my collection as if he'd just noticed it. "That's a lot of trophies."

"They are reminders," I told him curtly. "Not trophies."

"Oh?"

In truth, many were indeed trophies taken from the Tributes. Others, the most impressive ones, were gifts from Daedalus and Icarus. But I had no wish to elaborate. Theseus would not take silence as an answer, though. I sighed. "A lot of them are things that could have killed me." My eyes were drawn to the thief's dagger discarded at my side on the bed and I told myself I'd find a special place for that one.

He chuckled. "Is that where I would end up? On your wall."

I tried to imagine Theseus' skeleton hanging from a peg. His skull laughing at me.

"Corpses make poor trophies. They stink. Even those of so-called heroes," I told him, then added, "In less than twenty-four hours, you'll be in the sewer. Make them count."

He did not smile then. His eyes turned dark and cold as obsidian and he said, "Oh, I will."

VII

Theseus cleared his throat. "Let me start by apologising for killing your father."

I frowned in incomprehension. "The white bull?"

"He was your father, was he not?"

"He was a bull," I replied contemptuously.

Theseus shrugged. "Maybe. He certainly looked like one. But Heracles thought he was a god trapped in animal flesh – a fated god. What are they called again? Wyrd, yes, that's it. He told me that was why he didn't kill him. He didn't want to interfere in another god's curse, lest his own become worse."

"Did he say which god?" I asked, curious despite myself. Wyrds were not common amongst Olympians. The curse was foreign, alien to their costumes and rarely used for obvious reasons. Gods are a vengeful bunch.

"Mnevis, I think."

I guffawed. "The bull god himself?" Stars, but Theseus had an ego on him. To kill a beast and then call himself a hero was one thing. To claim to have slain a god – fated or no – was something else. I wonder if he'd even considered the fate of a godslayer.

"He was a bull," I repeated, unwilling to pander to his vanity. "A magnificent bull sent by Poseidon to test Minos. And I'm the one paying the price of his failure." Theseus looked sceptical. "Gods are like that, didn't you know? They care not who pays, as long as someone does."

"Is that how you see yourself?" he asked. "A victim?"

I frowned again. Then scowled. "Do you think I chose to be like this? Half bull, half man. Born of bestiality and adultery, fated to dwell here in this dungeon my entire life. Forced to fight for it every moon? Bah!" It was pointless to explain to the privileged hero the realities of a monster's misfortune, and so I bit my tongue to silence myself.

"You're closer to a daemon than a monster," he said, sniffing the cheese dubiously.

I expressed my contempt for his opinion with a forced exhale, too tired to tell him that, to a mortal, they are one and the same. Now I wish I hadn't been so blinded by disdain and hostility, or I might have asked him to elaborate on that comment.

Confident he wasn't going to go anywhere or shoot me in the back, for he was clearly having too much fun targeting me with words, I finally began tending to the cursed wound. He observed my every motion with a scholar's fascination. I wished he wouldn't. It's very unsettling to have eyes on you the entire time. I was used to being gawked at, but not actually observed. He rested his head on his wrist and pursed his lips in contemplation, suppressing what looked suspiciously like a genuinely amused smile.

"What?" I snapped. Of all reactions I'd triggered in humans, amusement had never been one of them.

"You're blond," he said.

"So?" said I, at a loss for why the red-haired hero

felt the need to point that out. Yellow hair – much like red – was indeed uncommon amongst the mortals in the Aegean, but I was no mere mortal and Mother had blonde hair too, or so I've been told.

"I had a cow once," he continued absently. "Well, technically, she belonged to my grandmother. Mimosa was her name – the cow, not my grandmother. It means cute or lovely and soft." He paused. "No, that's not quite right. It's hard to translate the meaning. There are so few words to describe fairness in this harsh language of yours." He puffed his cheeks. "What I'm trying to say is that she was the gentlest creature I've ever known… and had the exact same shade of hair as you."

I stared at him intently, unsure if he was giving me a compliment or an insult. "What are you getting at?"

His eyes became distant. "One day, priests from an obscure sect of the southern kingdom of the pyramids landed on our shore. They came to our village and slaughtered her in sacrifice to Mnevis – their god – who they'd claimed had vanished from their pantheon. They suspected foul play from the Olympians and so had been searching for him along the Aegean, sacrificing innocent creatures in their path to get the gods' attention. No one dared to stop them, not even the king." His upper lip curled as he spoke. "I was only a boy then, but old enough to understand that if I was ever going to triumph in the world of men, I needed the patronage of a god. And so I turned my grief and resentment into prayer. I chose to become a hero so I wouldn't be a victim."

I took a long hard look at him then. "That is the difference between us, *hero*. I never had a choice. Not even a chance. Do you believe people would applaud your deeds and think you clever and virtuous if you looked like me? To them, I'm a monster. A beast. I may be half man, half bull, but no matter what I do, the bull part is all people will ever see." I grunted my outrage and, fuck, I did sound like one.

He kept contemplating me as I unwrapped the linen from my side, his head tilted quizzically. "Hardly bovine at all, really," he mused, taking a bite of the cheese. "I mean, apart from the horns, the long face, the nose, the legs… and, of course, the hooves. Meh…" He waved a hand in a way that conveyed both dismissiveness and annoyance.

"What do you mean by" – I mimicked the infuriating gesture – "meh?!"

"I expected a monster, that's all." He moved to the fruit basket, put down the cheese, licking his lips in distaste, and selected a peach. I could have attacked him then, as he turned his back to me. But I was too slow to think. Slower even to act. No one had ever talked to me like that, not even Daedalus. Few ever talked to me at all. And there was a part of me that, yes, would rather talk than kill. Even with one such as Theseus.

"You're saying I'm not monstrous enough for you, is that it?" I said. I shouldn't have been offended, and yet that's exactly how I felt.

He took a bite out of the fruit and, apparently satisfied with it, sat back on the chair. "Gods and mortals have very different definitions of monstrosity," he said, chewing. "I've met satyrs more bestial than you." Another bite; juice spilled over his chin, down his throat, and onto his chest. He chased the juice to his navel with his middle finger, then licked it, utterly unaware of my murderous musings.

I let the insult slide. After a lifetime wondering what it would be like to be treated as an ordinary being, I confess I was disconcerted and more than a bit aggravated by the experience. I had bigger troubles at that moment, though. The linen had stuck fast to the cauterised flesh. The very idea of pulling on it made me flinch. To distract myself, I asked, "Where did you meet these satyrs?"

He kept chewing as he answered, "Does it matter?"

"No. I suppose not," I admitted with a muffled grunt. For it really didn't. Being compared to a satyr was almost as bad as being compared to a cow. Except far more accurate, I suppose.

With an effort of will, I pulled the top layer of linen from my skin. Pinpricks of light flooded my vision, and I felt dizzy again. Daedalus once told me people called these lights 'stars'. Not sure why. I'd always imagined stars to be brighter, steady and painless to look at. Regardless, those were the only stars I'd seen and would ever see alive. And with them still shining behind my eyes I exhaled, unwilling and not far from unable to continue the torturous task.

"You need to change that bandage," Theseus said, pointing at it with his little finger as he held the peach to his mouth again.

"What the fuck do you think I'm doing?"

"Looks to me you've lost your nerve and you're thinking of reasons not to." He wasn't wrong. "Here, let me do it for you."

"No!" I exclaimed vehemently. The very idea of him touching me only brought forth more stars, burning brightly with vexation and revulsion.

He lifted his hands in a placating gesture. "Hey, I'm just trying to help. I want us to have a fair fight and right now I could kill you where you sit."

He might have been right about that, too. Stars, I felt so weak. My body just kept getting weaker. It wasn't just exhaustion and lack of sleep. I felt the very life force draining out of me. I'd lost blood, sure, but not enough to cause this. I should have recovered by now. And could not ignore the fact that I hadn't. In any case, showing weakness in front of the hero just would not do, so I ripped the rest of the bandage off in one go with a mighty curse. Sure enough, the wound tore open and started bleeding again. The stars exploded in a bright outburst of agony.

"That was stupid," he said.

And didn't I know it. My hands shook as I outstretched them towards Daedalus' concoction, just slightly out of reach. I tried to stand. Failed. My legs would not stop trembling. I coughed and, having covered my mouth with the used cloth, saw that there was more fresh blood there than dried.

I understood the gravity of my situation then. In hindsight, I had known it much earlier, probably since that blade pierced my lung. I was bleeding internally and I would die like a star crushed by its own gravity. I remember thinking, *I'm supposed to die by the blade of a hero.* But the hero had come too late. I was already dead.

I shook my head. *No. Not dead yet,* I told myself. Daedalus would save me. He'd have some medicine or design a contraption to heal me. He'd have to. I couldn't die. *Not like this!*

Theseus saw me staring at the bloody cloth, spit out the peach seed into the sewer pit with remarkable accuracy and, sucking each fingertip one by one, came to my aid. I tried to stand again in protest.

"Stay down and let me do that before you rip out a rib, you big ox."

Too stunned to object, too lightheaded to move away, too tired to fight, I watched in a sort of daze as he crouched between me and the medicine chest, curious to see what he'd do next. I winced when his fingers touched my torso. Unlike Daedalus, his touch was light but firm. Not gentle, mind, but considerate, suitable for the task. His actions sure and precise. He acted with the practice of one who'd done this sort of thing many times before.

"You are a healer," I ventured.

"Hardly," he snorted. "I've just had a lot of practice mending flesh over the years."

This close, I could see his scars clearly. There were many – from scrapes to deep cuts and burns caused by both fire and rope. I fought it, but I couldn't help feeling a sort of respect for the warrior in this man and wondered if the circumstances had been different, might we have been friends rather than mortal enemies.

And that's when I realised that whatever happened, I was going to lose. For my death would give him glory whether or not he killed me himself. While his death would only give me more heroes to kill.

"Why are you doing this?" I asked in a voice low enough to be called a whisper.

"I already told you. I want a fair fight and I'd like to know you better before I kill you. Make no mistake, I *will* kill you. But I wish to understand who I'm killing first, and why they want you dead so badly."

My ears perked up. "Who's they?"

He paused. Only for a moment, but long enough for me to perceive he had not wished to reveal this secret. Something he was both afraid and ashamed of.

"Gods," he murmured uncomfortably. Likely concerned they might be listening. I remembered what he'd said about having the favour of the gods and wondered now which ones.

"Tell me the truth, please. After all, where's the harm? You'll kill me afterwards, no matter what, right?" I said.

He smiled, but it had no mirth in it, no wickedness, not even a hint of that self-assured glibness that seemed to define the man. "What do you know of Troezen?" he asked conversationally while he worked.

"Nothing. Never even heard of the place until yesterday," I admitted.

"It lies on the northeastern Peloponnese coast. A stretch of land stuck between Sparta and Athens. A neutral kingdom – by necessity, not choice – acting as a buffer between those two major powers, too unimportant and poor to be coveted by either but unable to grow or take sides, lest they change their minds. The peculiar geography and political situation kept us isolated and safe from plunder. Not that there's much to plunder, but… that never stopped those intent on it."

I nodded, inferring both agreement and incentive to continue.

"On the surface, it's not much different from this island," he continued. "It has the same type of trees, same wildflowers, same crops, seasons, and animals. We worship the same gods – Poseidon above all. The people, though, are quite different."

He was different, all right. Taller, leaner and sharper than the average human. But there was also a darkness around him, like an aura, absorbing the firelight. Again, I considered what Icarus had said, that he was soulless. Now that I've seen that darkness in others, I recognise it as the manifestation of a will so strong and unyielding it might as well be a singularity itself, capturing everything and everyone in its path. And it wasn't greed in his eyes, but hunger. Hunger for power; not for power's sake, but for the resources, options, agency and opportunities it brought to those who wielded it. Theseus was a man on a quest. Killing was not the goal, only a means to an end. I would find out which one.

The wound cleaned, he began winding the bandage as he spoke. He told me of his childhood, growing under the weight of his mother's resentment and his grandfather's indifference. Of his friends, herders and fishermen who, despite having no title or property, still fought for their land. And of Aegeus, who he despised more than Minos.

This catharsis proved he had no intention of letting me live.

"There, that should hold for another day or so," he said after he finished.

"Thank you," I said, impressed with his work. *Perhaps now it will heal*, I lied to myself.

Before he got up, I gripped his shoulder, keeping

him from standing so we remained face to face. I wanted to see his reaction to my next question up close.

"What about the gods?" I asked. For clearly he'd rather tell me his life story than mention them again.

He feigned incomprehension.

"Those who want me dead. The ones you prayed to." It did not take Daedalus' genius to figure out they had to be the same ones.

I felt his tension and rage through my grip. If hate carried an electrical current, I'd have been burned to a crisp. I released him, for he would not answer otherwise.

He stood up, chewed on his lip for a moment, then spat the next words at me. "I prayed to a Chronodéndron, alright!"

I blinked a few times. "What the fuck is a Chronodéndron?"

"A tree. As ancient as it is sentient."

"I've never seen a tree," I said truthfully, without thinking. And the only creatures I knew of that even remotely resembled a sentient tree were dryads. But they did not listen to prayers, only praises.

"May you never see one of these," he said miserably. "I was young and angry and desperate. I'd prayed to the gods first, but none of them cared. Not even Poseidon – I don't believe he is my father, by the way," he admitted with resentful candour. "I'm not even sure Aegeus is, so dissimilar are we of features, but I figured it wouldn't hurt to be thought of as the son of a god as well as a king. Maybe that's why he never answered my prayers…" he reflected bitterly, then set his jaw. "So I turned to the tree."

Ignorance is not something one admits to lightly,

but I really had no idea what type of tree he was talking about.

"How does this tree have the power to answer prayers?" I said in my most patient and friendly tone.

He grimaced. "Not prayers – wills. Chronodéndrons are Chronos' weapons against the Fates."

"Chronos? The god of time? Why would *he* need them?" After all, Chronos was renowned for being the most powerful god in the Universe. Even Zeus couldn't get to his level and the stars knew he kept trying.

"Everyone has enemies," Theseus said simply, making himself comfortable on the bed next to me.

Then the full meaning of his words sank in. "And he wants *me* dead?! Why?"

It made no sense. Then again, little about the gods ever did.

"He wants me to kill you, yes. At least I assume it's him. Chronodéndrons speak for no other deity. As to why… ," he continued rather apologetically. "At first, I thought he didn't care one way or the other. That you were only a means to achieve my ends. I needed to become a hero and in order to do that, I had to kill a monster. It made sense."

"For fuck's sake!" Only to a god, a hero or a madman would this reasoning make sense.

He held up his hands defensively. "But then another god, one I had not prayed to – no one does – came to me and asked me to kill you in exchange for something quite exorbitant. So now that I've met you, I'm not so sure about Chronos' intent. But it makes no difference. I'll do what I have to do to fulfil my end of the bargain with him and I won't ask your forgiveness, for I expect none. I've made my choice. I just need you to know it's nothing personal."

It felt very personal to me, but I tried to remain reasonable. "What other god?"

"That I cannot tell you. I'm sworn to silence."

"Then at least tell me what exactly you have willed with your prayer to the tree. I doubt it included this." I gestured at us, sitting across from each other, conversing in the hearth of the Labyrinth like old friends.

He smiled wryly, dark eyes glinting with wickedness once again. "My prayers are my business. Take comfort in the fact I, too, am cursed to pay for this prayer with both my mortal life and my immortal soul."

The sincerity of his words matched their finality. I wanted to ask more. Wanted to rage, to shout in his face and demand, if not an explanation, at least an apology for being so rudely and unfairly involved in the gods' schemes. As if Minos' ambitions weren't enough… But what would be the point? We are all pawns in the gods' games, even they themselves.

Silence fell and with it a melancholy so strong I could almost believe we were both dead, outside time and realm, navigating our own personal mazes of cause and consequence.

Then anger flared again.

"I might be one with horns and hooves, but you are the real monster, Theseus. You chose to curse yourself and those around you because you wanted praise and power and glory and, as you said, you like to kill. Blame the gods all you want; blame me as well while you're at it. Phah! You're fooling no one but yourself – *hero*."

He regarded me with curiosity and a vestige of something like sympathy. "Why do you kill?"

"I kill because otherwise they'd kill me, you arrogant arse!"

"Why not let them?"

"Are you mocking me now?"

"No. It's a valid question. If you hate killing so much. If you hate your life. Then why fight? Why have you not let them end it long ago?"

Pride, mostly, I thought. But I did not tell him that. Instead I got up and said: "Because I may be the embodiment of their flaws, the product of adultery and rape. The monstrous beast they are allowed to hurt and hate. But I will not be their trophy – or yours. I choose to live, even if I have to kill for it."

To my surprise, he grinned. "So you, too, made a choice. It's a shitty choice, don't get me wrong, but it's still a choice. Sometimes those are the only ones available to men like us. Don't blame me if the difference between a hero and a monster is simply a matter of perspective. We're two sides of the same coin, you and I."

Men like us, he'd said. I was so taken aback by this, I couldn't think of an appropriate response.

Theseus moved to stand on top of the sewer grate. "Have you ever tried to escape?" he asked, looking down. "You might have succeeded if you had."

"What would be the point? The Labyrinth wasn't built to protect humanity from me. But me from humanity."

He nodded gravely. "So you understand."

"Yes, I understand humanity very well. I care

nothing for it," I said. And in that moment I realised it was true.

"What about the poor women and slaves who are sent here to die? Have you ever tried talking to any of them? Or let any of them go?"

"No," I admitted. "They were all too busy screaming, running around or trying to kill me. My curiosity never quite exceeded my patience." And I wondered, had I tried to talk to the Amazon, the priestesses or the man lost in the maze, would things have turned out differently? I quickly put the thought away. Things might have turned out differently all right, but not better. There was no real escape. No way out. Not for me, nor for them. Then it hit me. "What do you think is going to happen after you kill me?" I asked him. "Minos only let you try because he knows that, whatever happens, you won't get out. No one does."

"I might," he said, still looking down the shaft.

"That sewer is not an exit," I told him. "If the fall doesn't kill you, it's over a mile of tunnel underwater. You'd drown."

He pondered this with a snort. "Like I said, bad choices are still choices."

He's insane, I thought. Utterly insane. "And what would be the point of risking my life giving them that choice when my entire purpose is to end theirs?"

"I don't know. But I'm not the one who claims to hate killing."

I groaned in exasperation. "I see what you're doing. It's easy for you to say that, to judge me, because you have never been hated. Never been hunted. Never been deprived of freedom or humanity. Talk, bah. No, I never saw the point of talking to those who only wanted to murder me."

"So what changed?" he asked condescendingly.

I thought about lying, but as far as I could tell, we were being fairly honest with each other and, in this case, my curiosity had exceeded my patience. I waited until his gaze fixed on mine again before I answered. "You could have killed me in my sleep. Or stabbed me in the back when I didn't even know you were there. Even now, you could probably reach for that spear on the wall and put my immortality to the test before I could react."

He nodded. "Yes, I could, but –" He tensed. "What was that?"

"Someone's coming."

VIII

"Asterius?" Icarus called through the wall. "Asterius, are you there?"

"Hide!" I did not have to tell Theseus twice. And I've never seen anyone move so fast! In just a few long strides, he was out of the room. I cursed inwardly, thinking now I'd have to chase him across the maze – again. But to my surprise, I saw his red hair poking from behind the corner, his eyes wide, darting from me to the wall. I put a finger to my lips and pulled the curtain hiding the window.

"Yes, Icarus."

"Why did you close the curtain?"

"Can't a monster have privacy?"

He actually pondered this. "I suppose… So, did you find her yet?"

"No." I lied. Well, technically, it was not a lie since Theseus wasn't a 'her'. And I really didn't want to have to explain my truce with the hero to the boy when I hardly understood it myself.

"So, why are you still here? You should be out looking for her!"

"I had to tend to my wound," I retorted, mildly offended by his tone. Icarus had never raised his voice to me. Never told me what to do. This must have come from Daedalus. He sounded just like his father in a pique of frustration.

"But –"

"I'm a monster, not a machine. I can't patrol the maze day and night like Talos. I have to eat and sleep and, more importantly, heal."

"But there's no time!"

"What? Why? Daedalus said I had a couple of days at least." And he'd either lied to me or he himself had been deceived, for after all, Theseus was already here.

"Not anymore," Icarus said bleakly. "Theseus vowed to only consummate the marriage once he'd killed you."

"Did he now?" I said, glancing sidelong to where Theseus stood, looking sheepish.

"Yes," the boy continued, getting agitated. "He refuses to court Ariadne or even see her. He's been secluded in his quarters, training day and night for the fight. I think it's bullshit – no offence. Father says he's likely to be in a brothel somewhere. Ariadne is of the same opinion. She thinks he's avoiding her and, fearing he's changed his mind about the marriage, abandoned all plans for a big wedding. She's now decided to marry at sunrise. She would have married at sunset, believe me, but even a hasty wedding needs a feast and food needs time to cook." He puffed his cheeks. "Everyone is already overworked and sleep deprived. The princess doesn't care, of course. All she cares about is herself and her party and losing her maidenhood, apparently."

I felt a blade cut deep into my heart, almost as painfully and vividly as the thief's blade between my ribs.

That implied Ariadne not only wanted Theseus to live, she wanted me dead. Or at the very least, was willing – eager! – to sacrifice my life for her pleasure. Maybe she believed I'd be better off dead… That's why she'd given him the thread. Under Daedalus' instruction or not, I reckon she'd spun it long ago and even dyed it the same colour as the stone, specifically for the purpose, for she knew that as long as I lived, the chances of her finding a husband or fame on her own were slim. I felt sick. My own sister didn't care about my suffering as long as her desires were fulfilled. I shouldn't have been surprised. And I hated that I felt so hurt, so betrayed. Tears gathered behind my eyes. I willed them to dry.

Monsters don't cry.

They do throw up, though.

"Oh, gods, Asterius! Are you all right?"

Clearly not, I thought, staring at bloody bile on the floor. "I'm fine," I said and sat down again before I fell over.

"You don't look fine…" the boy whispered.

"It's your father's concoction. It doesn't agree with my stomach. That's all."

"Are you sure?"

"Yes." I swallowed hard and cleared my throat until I was sure my voice wouldn't break. "Very well. Let him come. I am ready."

"But the priestess –" started Icarus.

"She's not a problem." Another half-lie at best. It's the thing with lying, once you start…

"So you have found her?" The boy's face expressed a different sort of distress now.

I cursed. This is why I never lie. I'm not good at it.

"Yes!" I admitted grudgingly. "I found her and I killed her. Accidentally!" I added before he thought even less of me.

Icarus eyed me keenly. "You said *is*. She *is* not a problem. Present tense. You're still lying!"

I could have howled. Curse the boy and his damned shrewdness. His father would be so proud.

"Fine! Yes, I found her, and like I said, she posed no threat, so I let her go."

"Where?" He shook himself. "Why?"

"Because she could have killed me," I admitted, too deep into the misunderstanding to bother with the right pronoun. "And she didn't."

His mouth hung open. "So you let her live?"

"Is that not reason enough to spare a life? What sort of monster do you think I am?" I asked, without giving him a chance to answer. "Besides, your father ordered me not to kill her."

"I bet he's regretting it now," he muttered. "Did you talk to her, at least?"

"Briefly," I replied cautiously.

"What did she say? Did she tell you who sent her? Did she tell you about the machines?"

I managed to keep my expression neutral at the first two questions, but the third bewildered me. My treacherous ears twitched involuntarily. Icarus' eyes widened and his breath caught, realising I had no idea what he was talking about. He enunciated his next words slowly and intently, as if trying to infuse them with a meaning beyond mere understanding.

"Asterius, you must find her again, and this time, you must kill her."

Try as I might, I could not fathom the reason behind Icarus' sudden and disproportionate alarm regarding this priestess. The very dissonance of events hindered hypothesis, and I failed to see any correlation between a foreign priestess and machines, of all things.

Yes, I already told you, I knew Icarus was building what he called a flying machine – able to fly high enough to take him to meet my grandfather, Helios, he'd once teased. The truth was, he hated boats and wished people were able to fly across the sea instead. But what in the stars had that to do with me? I wasn't flying anywhere. Sure, I wondered what else he and his father had been up to. And if anyone could build a person it would be Daedalus. But like I said, it should have nothing to do with me. And remember, Theseus had assured me he'd killed the priestess.

No, Theseus was no machine. Yes, I'm certain. How? Because he ate – a lot! Because blood flowed in his veins, breath filled in his lungs. He might not have been entirely human – that much I gathered from his cunning mind and speed of movement. Maybe he was indeed a demigod, or more likely, gifted by a god. After all, a gift is just another word for curse, as Daedalus used to say. But he was no machine, of that much, at least, I was certain.

Anyway, while my mind reeled in search of a reply, Icarus' earnestness turned to contempt.

"She got to you, didn't she?" he said. "What did she do? What did she offer you? Freedom, revenge, sex… *love*?"

I shook my head, hung low in frustration and

embarrassment while Theseus sniggered quietly around the corner. "You're talking nonsense, Icarus."

"You're the one not listening to sense! Asterius, Father says she's a harbinger of death. A creature of the Underworld, maybe a daemon. Or worse!"

I'd had enough. "Well, he would know, wouldn't he? Since he was the one who sent her here!"

The boy paled. "What?"

I drew in a deep breath, grasping for patience. "He sent that priestess here. She had a triggerbow and a glass eye able to see in the dark."

"No! He wouldn't. Those items were stolen."

"Bullshit."

"It's true!"

"What about the yarn? Maybe Ariadne stole it along with the idea, huh?"

He blinked in confusion. "I-I don't know what yarn you're talking about, but the bow and the eye, they were stolen by Theseus – or his men, it makes no difference. Asterius, you have to believe me! That's what I came here to tell you. To warn you. It's why you have to find her first. Before –" He covered his mouth, eyes opened wide. "Oh no. He got to her first, didn't he? He's already here, with you!"

I glanced at Theseus and he grinned. It was the most self-assured and wicked grin I'd ever seen. Much like the one you're giving me now. The grin of a hunter, pleased with the prey caught in his trap.

"Before what?" I asked, without answering, all but confirming his deduction.

Icarus winced. He did not reply. He did not have to,

for there it was, loud and clear, the thing neither father nor son would admit, that even they believed Theseus would best me. Talk about fate…

The boy lowered his eyes, then took a deep breath. "Asterius, listen to me: The priestess had something of great power – a weapon, I think. Maybe she hid it. Maybe it doesn't look like a weapon. I don't know what it looks like… only that it's powerful and dangerous. You must find it before Theseus does. It's important!" He made it sound like the fate of the universe rested on it.

"Why?" I asked.

"I can't tell you…" He actually looked ashamed.

"You better tell me something, Icarus. First, Father wants me to catch this woman for interrogation. Then it seems he no longer needs or wants the information, so I must kill her instead without questioning her or his motives. Now that she's dead, I must find some item that you can't even describe and remain ignorant about what it is or what it does." A rebellious growl grew within me. "I deserve better than that."

"Yes!" he said. His face beaming with hope. "Yes, Asterius, you deserve to live!"

"Damn right I do!"

He bit his lip. "But we don't always get what we deserve…"

I guffawed. A mirthless, verging on the manic sound of contempt. Stars, he knew. Icarus knew I would die that day.

Once I managed to control my emotions, I ruminated on his words for a long moment, desperately trying to understand, to make sense of all this. I couldn't. Not sure I have, even now. Finally, I reasserted myself and hardened to the conclusion that it made no difference. Nothing had changed, really. I was a monster. Monsters are meant to be killed. The only way I'd survived thus far was by killing all who entered the Labyrinth. No exceptions. It was foolish of me to try otherwise. To… wish otherwise. Even when my own life was forfeited. For indeed, it was. I felt it dwindling with every breath, every heartbeat. I considered asking the boy to fetch his father to help me, or at least explain what had happened. But what would be the point? Had Daedalus wanted to enlighten me on what the fuck was going on, he'd have done so already. And then I realised Daedalus must have known the extent of my injury the moment he saw it. How could he not? He understood anatomy better than anyone. Either he would not or could not heal me. All his concoction had done was numb both my pain and my brain long enough for me to complete his task. My last task. That was no task at all, for another had already completed it.

I set my jaw and said through clenched teeth, "Go away, Icarus. Leave me alone."

I pulled the curtain closed with such force, I nearly ripped it off the rail. That was the last time I saw that boy's face. He called out a few times half-heartedly, then urged me once again to be careful and bid me good luck. It sounded like a farewell. Which, I suppose, it was.

I still don't know what had happened during that night to cause the sudden change of plans as well as the change of heart. Even Icarus, I later realised, had changed. He'd looked different, darker… older. Back then, I'd assumed it was because he was anxious and exhausted with the wedding preparations, but now… well, as it turns out, I'm only a bad liar to others. To myself, I'm as good as you.

Theseus resumed his place in the chair once Icarus' retreating steps faded and the curtain was fastened in place.

"Asterius. Is that your name?" he asked in amazement.

I stared. "Yes. Didn't you know that?" A sudden suspicion came to mind. "Don't people know my name?!"

"Everyone calls you the Minotaur."

My fists clenched; my whole body tensed with rage. Of course, Minos would not have shared my real name. The best way to turn a being into a thing is to take away their name, replace it with a moniker that reflects someone's ownership over them.

"It's a lovely name," Theseus said before I could punch something. "Fit for a god," he added with a smile that was both enigmatic and pragmatic and utterly disarming.

"Don't," I said, pinching the bridge of my nose.

"What?" he replied, pretending innocence.

"Don't try to distract me or flatter me, or whatever it is you're doing. You heard what he said. He knows you're here, so, come on, the weapon or whatever it is Daedalus wants, give it to me." I stretched out my hand.

He raised his. "I've no idea what he was talking about, I swear." He pointed to his naked self. "I have nothing else on me, as you can see."

"I don't have time to play games! I have to kill you before the night is out."

"Wrong. *I* have to kill *you*. Otherwise, I'd miss my own wedding," he replied playfully. "Believe me, I'd rather stay here and talk some more, for I have no interest in marriage, especially to Ariadne." Distaste on the verge of repulsion tainted his buoyancy. "But a promise is a promise, for gods and heroes both. We are nothing without our promises." He must have seen the judgement on my face and feigned contrition before saying with a glint of mischief, "Fear not. I won't be cruel to the girl. I won't even have a chance to."

"What do you mean by that?"

"She's not my prize. Only the price of the prize." He winked.

For what? To whom? I wondered. "Eh?" I said.

He waved his hand, abandoning all pretence. That dark aura surrounded him when he spoke. His tone sombre. "Doesn't matter. Her time will come. Ours, sadly, is at an end."

I puffed my cheeks. In my rage, I'd forgotten to ask Icarus how long I had until dawn. Hours surely, but… how many? Again, I had to remind myself that it made no difference. Our fate was indeed sealed. Better to get it over with while I was still strong enough to crush his skull.

He turned his back to me and peeked behind the curtain, bending his torso into the window as if trying to fit through. How easy it would be to kill him then. I got the feeling he knew it too. He was testing me, giving me a chance – a choice. Fate always gives you a choice. That's why she's so cruel.

"Is Daedalus the one who named you?" Theseus asked, back still turned.

"I'm not sure," I said truthfully. "I assume he did. The stars know my real parents didn't."

"Is that why you call him Father?"

"Yes. In my heart, he is my true father. The only father I've ever known. He raised me. Cared for me. He –"

"Built this cage for you," Theseus interjected, turning around.

"What else could he have done?"

"Killed you. Sent you away. He chose to keep you and use you."

"Minos uses me. Not him."

"Are you sure?"

"What are you getting at?"

"The truth," he said plainly. "Daedalus' name travels far and wide and carries more weight than Minos himself. They say he's the most gifted, most intelligent man that ever lived. They say he's gifted by gods – not *the* gods, do you understand? Some say Prometheus, others Hephaestus. Others claim it's by both! But my favourite rumour is that he is, in fact, the pawn of a vengeful goddess. A goddess from another pantheon. Has been so since his wife died. They say he creates life out of metal and gemstones through magic, not genius. I've met the man. And I believe *they* might be right. Now, why would a man like that be content with a subordinate position to a lesser man?"

"Minos is a king," I said lamely.

"Ah, yes. But a king who, like most kings, is only king in name. Everyone in the Aegean knowns who really runs things. Don't you?"

I confess this was too much for me right then. The paradigm shift in thought too great to follow, to comprehend, let alone accept. And so I just stared at him while his words deconstructed everything I'd called true and real and sane in life.

I started seeing stars again, felt lightheaded and had to sit back down. I sat on the bed, nearly cutting myself on the thief's blade, partially hidden in the folds of the quilt.

The blade that killed me, I said to myself as I picked it up for one last look before putting it on the wall with the others and once again wondered how I could have been brought down by something so small, so insignificant. Then I noticed the amber had changed. Before, it had almost seemed to shine with a light of its own. Now many little dark blobs swirled inside the resin, like oil on water, turning it murky and dull. I held it up to the nearest flame for a better look.

"Where did you get that?" Theseus asked, an odd strain in his voice.

My hand involuntarily reached for the wound. "This is the blade that stabbed me."

He practically leapt to my side and snatched it from my hand.

His face turned pale. "This is not a mortal's blade."

For some reason, seeing him holding the dagger irked me and I took it from his hand as swiftly as he'd snatched it from mine and a great deal rougher. "The one who had it was mortal enough, believe me," I told him.

"The thief!" he cried.

"He was your man?!" I practically growled the question, ready to stab him.

"No! The priestess... She said – oh, gods – she told

me a thief had taken her dagger, but I thought nothing of it."

"You knew each other?"

He rubbed his face. "Not exactly. She came to me, asked for my help in return for a way inside the Labyrinth. It was she who'd suggested we replace the Tributes. She needed me to kill the slave and get rid of the body, you see. But Ariadne had told me you did not kill women, so I killed the poor slave and instead of killing one of the men for me to replace, I killed the priestess, too."

The silence that followed lasted a long moment.

"I cannot believe this," I finally said. "What sort of hero are you? Killing innocent women –" I heard the hypocrisy in my argument the moment I spoke it.

He glared at me. "As if you have not! Don't you dare judge me. The slave might have been innocent, but if I hadn't killed her, you would have. The priestess was not innocent, I assure you. Her intentions had to be wicked. She said she only wanted to talk to you. That afterwards, I could kill you. She even said you wouldn't put up a fight after she was done with you! She was one of them – the priests who killed my cow – that's why I killed her." His voice dwindled to a near whimper. He glanced at the dagger again and cursed. "She was desperate for her weapon, though. I would be too."

"What is so special about this dagger, Theseus?" I asked. But once again, I somehow knew the answer before he gave it to me.

"This wood came from a Chronodéndron. And the soulstone...."

"The what?" A coughing fit took hold of me, likely triggered by emotion. This time I could not conceal the blood.

Theseus' mouth fell slightly agape, gaze darting from the blade to the blood and back to me. He gasped. "No. No! Oh gods, no!"

This dramatic display of denial had little to do with my well-being. His horror came from the realisation he'd been denied the glory of a fair fight and an honourable kill.

"Who did this? Where's the man who stabbed you?" he asked urgently.

I winced towards the sewer. "He was a thief. Like she said. Just a simple thief who got lucky with a slight of hand attack."

He kept shaking his head, looking more wounded than I felt. "No. It can't be. It makes no sense."

"I'm dying, Theseus. You came too late." There was no triumph in my voice, no vindication of any sort, only sadness and regret.

"No!" he protested, as if I'd slapped him. "You can't die. You must live. I'm the one who kills you. Me!"

I could have laughed. "And who would know otherwise? Take the glory for yourself, Theseus. I no longer care." It was the truth. The melancholy of previous days, combined with the recent events, had turned into a depression so great, I'd begun to welcome death without even realising. And, now that I had, I also realised I'd rather go down in history as being killed by a hero than a common thief.

"No. You don't understand. *I* must kill you. It is written. I must… Otherwise… Oh gods! We are doomed."

"Who's we?"

"Mankind."

I chuckled at his exaggeration. "There will be other monsters to kill, Theseus. And like I said… you can claim your victory to the world. I won't tell. And besides, just because something is written doesn't make it true."

No, Daedalus didn't say that. I did.

"It should have been me," Theseus said with such sorrow I wished he had been the one to kill me. Then something occurred to me and I knew exactly what to do. "Here." I gave him the dagger.

He blinked. I nodded.

He gaped, but he accepted the blade with steady hands.

He then knelt by the bed, head down, almost in prayer. When he lifted it again, I saw he had tears in his eyes. "It was not supposed to be like this," he said through gritted teeth.

"I've been telling myself that same thing since the moment you walked into the Labyrinth." I tried to chuckle and triggered another bloody coughing fit instead. Stars, I hardly had any breath left in me.

Theseus shook his head. "There's no happy ending for men like us in this world," he said. It sounded like he was quoting someone, but I didn't ask who. For there it was again: *men like us*. I might have been a monster, but he saw only a man. And so how could I have killed the only one who ever saw me for who I am?

I squeezed his fingers around the blade's handle. "Finish it," I whispered.

He held up the dagger in one hand, cupped my nape in the other, and looked straight into my eyes. "The gods fooled us both, Asterius. But I'll make sure the world will always remember your name. You'll become more famous than your father, your mother, the king, your sister, or" – he stopped to clear his throat – "or even me. That I promise you." The gem on the handle glowed slightly, almost imperceptibly, like a candle about to flicker out. "We'll meet again in the under-world, brother," he said. "Until then, tell Hades he's a cunt."

In one swift and precise motion, Theseus plunged the blade into my neck, severing the main artery. Blood gushed from my throat like the ichor from Talos' ankle.

I tried to smile, to be serene and brave, but I shook and cried out because in that moment I'd had traded any fame for one more breath of life. One more glimpse of flame. One more sound. One more touch. One more anything… but there was none.

There was nothing but darkness.

IX

"So… that's it. My death's story, if you will."

"Indeed. Quite the tale – no pun intended."

"Spare me, Hades. You promised me that if I told you how I died, you would tell me everything that happened afterwards."

"Not everything. *Everything* would take an eternity to tell."

"It's a good thing we have eternity, then, Lord of the Underworld."

"That's the problem, Asterius, scion of Helios… we don't. I'll tell you what happened to those you cared about. That was what I promised you."

"Very well. Go on."

"After he put you out of your misery, Theseus left the Labyrinth the way he'd entered, carrying your head as a trophy. Daedalus himself opened the door and thanked him. Minos welcomed him with open arms, like a son. He married Ariadne that very sunrise, your blood still on his hands, and immediately set sail without consummating the marriage. Then he abandoned her in Naxos where Dionysus waited."

"Dionysus? Stars! That's awful. Ariadne wronged me, true. But… why, of all the princesses in the world, would he want her?"

"My guess is because she's also the granddaughter of a Titan of light. And after the initial shock – and a lot of bawling, I imagine – she learned to love the beast. Ain't that ironic?"

"Humph."

"Theseus himself became very famous, the epitome of heroism. But not happy. And, as he foresaw, never more famous than you or the Labyrinth. Not many followed in his footsteps, either. There were no more monsters to kill, you see. But there were plenty of bulls. And so heroism became a sport, a spectacle for the weak and narrow-minded."

"I don't understand."

"Ah, right. Let me elaborate. Icarus told you Theseus taunted the white bull – who, yes, was a fated god, but that's another story – but he did not describe how. It was quite clever, actually, in a sadistic sort of way. Whenever the bull charged him, Theseus would leap over it and stab him as he charged by. He did this again and again until the poor beast, unable to overcome its instincts, grew tired and bled out. The crowds loved it. So much so they made a sport of it. Bulls were taunted, tortured and slaughtered for entertainment for millennia after that. Many preferred it to the theatre, in fact. Because you see, to the masses, cruelty is fun. Without it, they don't feel included. They need to see, to experience the violence first hand from the sidelines and project themselves in the place of the aggressor – or what they then call the hero. The very concepts of bravery and valour, virtue and vice, or simple good versus evil, have gotten pretty twisted over the ages."

"Ages? How long has passed?"

"Oh… that depends. Time is, er…relative."

"You know what? I don't care. What about Icarus? Did he ever get to fly?"

"Ah… that he did. He became quite famous as well, for all it's worth."

"What happened?"

"He tried to reach the sun, as he said he would. But his wings were assembled with beeswax and they melted. He fell from the sky, plunged into the sea, and drowned."

"No… poor Icarus. He'd always been afraid of the sea… That's why he wanted to fly."

"Precisely."

"Why didn't the gods intervene?"

"They did, after a fashion. By not interfering, that is. And no, I had nothing to do with it. I rarely leave my realm. Daedalus knew there would be a price to pay for his hubris and misuse of the gifts he'd been given. But like most men, he did not expect it to be so high, or that someone else might have to pay in his stead. We gods are not fussy about where the payment comes from, as long as we get our due. As you said."

"So he was gifted, then. That's disappointing. I always believed Daedalus was naturally brilliant – a fluke of humanity."

"You were half correct. His intelligence was not a gift. Other things were… the Labyrinth, for example."

"You mean –"

"Oh, please. How could a single man have built something on that scale?"

"I… I never really thought about it."

"Of course not. No one did. It was part of the 'gift'.

Anyway, he'd been unstable since his wife's death and went completely mad after Icarus fell. He vowed to destroy the gods for what they'd done to his son."

"If any mortal could, it would be him."

"Exactly. He hasn't stopped trying. Things being what they are, he might even succeed."

"How so?"

"Have you ever heard of the Nephilim?"

"No. The name means nothing to me."

"Are you sure?"

"Yes. I knew he'd had dealings with gods, but he never told me which ones. Besides, you're the one who brought me back to life and restored my memories, so you tell me."

"I did not restore your memories, only your conscience. And you were never truly dead, only… dormant. Death is such an ugly word. Its definition forced by the limitations of the mortal perspective. You were no mere mortal to begin with, and so you were only in another state of being."

"My body died. I'm sure of it. I felt it."

"A minor technicality for beings like us. I made sure your soul was kept intact."

"How?"

"With this."

"The thief's dagger! How did you – I mean, Theseus had it, so how –"

"That's another story, not part of our deal. All I'll say now is that it never belonged to the thief. He stole it from that ungodly priestess in exchange for a blissful existence in the Underworld. What? That's what thieves do; they steal things. Don't look so appalled. He was going to die anyway, so I made him a bargain. That's what gods do. And he was no ordinary thief. He was the best pickpocket of his age. I've forgotten his name… oh, well. Who cares? He's dead. But this, oh, this is no ordinary dagger either. With this I managed to – how to put it – pluck you out of time. You're welcome, by the way."

"Why?"

"Because you, my friend, are a star. And we need as many of those as we can get."

"For what?"

"To cast a shadow."

"Huh?"

"It will make sense eventually, I promise."

"Right… Are you going to put my soul into a rotting corpse now?"

"Do not insult me. I'm not Anubis! You'll have a proper body, just like your old one – as is befitting of your soul. Unless you prefer something less aggravating to the mortal senses? That too can be arranged. I won't judge. The stars know I've changed aspects many times and for far less worthy reasons."

"No. Thank you for the offer, but I am what I am and I'm proud of it. It took me long enough to realise that."

"Excellent."

"One more thing: Why did Theseus call you a cunt?"

"Maybe because I am. Or can be. Have to be, often enough. It's part of being a god. Also why we get fucked so often, I reckon. Let's just say being a god is not much different from being a monster."

"I find that hard to believe."

"Well, my friend, if anyone will ever be able to testify to that statement, it will be you. Shall we begin?"

"I want to see Theseus first. Is he here?"

"I'm afraid not."

"Is he not dead?"

"Sort of…"

"Tell me where he is."

"… with the Nephilim."

"Are those the machines Icarus mentioned?"

"Ah, good. You're finally catching up. Now, for the last time, come with me. We have much to do. And the only chance you have of ever seeing your hero again is if we do it before Time reasserts itself."

"I have no idea what that means, but sure, let's cast the greatest shadow the Universe has ever seen."

"That's my monster."